The interv...
well.

He pushed the ...
threshold. His ...
his mouth felt ...
somewhere far away, he dredged up his voice.

'Emily. . .'

Like an old movie, frame by frame, heartbeat
by heartbeat, she lifted her head and met his
eyes.

'David. . .'

He hadn't changed at all. . .

Dear Reader

In Caroline Anderson's ONCE MORE, WITH FEELING, Emily and David meet again after their divorce, in HEART ON THE LINE Jean Evans' Georgia goes to Ethiopia after a broken engagement, and in Australia Meredith Webber's Elly has A DIFFERENT DESTINY. We're very pleased to introduce new author Josie Metcalfe, whose Rebecca and Alex have NO ALTERNATIVE but to respond to each other. With such good reading, how could you not have a wonderful Christmas? Enjoy!

The Editor

!!!STOP PRESS!!! If you enjoy reading these medical books, have you ever thought of writing one? We are always looking for new writers for LOVE ON CALL, and want to hear from you. Send for the guidelines, with SAE, and start writing!

Caroline Anderson's nursing career was brought to an abrupt halt by a back injury, but her interest in medical things led her to work first as a medical secretary, and then after completing her teacher training, as a lecturer in Medical Office Practice to trainee medical secretaries. In addition to writing, she also runs her own business from her home in rural Suffolk, where she lives with her husband, two daughters, mother and assorted animals.

Recent titles by the same author:

NOTHING LEFT TO GIVE
ROLE PLAY

ONCE MORE, WITH FEELING

BY

CAROLINE ANDERSON

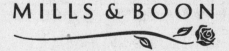

MILLS & BOON

MILLS & BOON LIMITED
ETON HOUSE, 18–24 PARADISE ROAD
RICHMOND, SURREY, TW9 1SR

For Mary, who made it, and for Rhea,
with many thanks for all the help

*MILLS & BOON, the Rose Device and LOVE ON CALL
are trademarks of the publisher.*

*First published in Great Britain 1994
by Mills & Boon Limited*

© Caroline Anderson 1994

*Australian copyright 1994   Philippine copyright 1994
This edition 1994*

ISBN 0 263 78883 0

*Set in 10 on 12 pt Linotron Times
03-9412-50384*

*Typeset in Great Britain by Centracet, Cambridge
Made and printed in Great Britain*

CHAPTER ONE

'AT LAST!'

Emily turned into the health centre car park and killed the engine, glancing at her watch with a sigh of relief. She still had three minutes to spare, but only by the grace of God.

With a wry grin she recalled the advert for the job.

'Four-partner practice in rural North Devon urgently needs full-time replacement partner because of unforeseen retirement due to ill health. Must be on obstetric list and do minor surgery, CHS and IUCD. Most important qualification an ability to map-read. . .'

They weren't kidding! She had meandered back and forth across Exmoor, which would have been lovely if she'd had time to appreciate the scenery, but she was determined not to be late.

The trouble was, the roads were all so tiny it was hard to tell which were major and which were minor. Assumptions, she had fast discovered, were a foolish luxury. Still, she was wise to their tricks now and read every single sign—hence her arrival with three—no, two now—minutes to go before her interview.

She had spoken on the phone to the senior partner, Dr Allen, who had sounded very welcoming and encouraging—or was that just wishful thinking on Emily's part? Whatever, she would still have to run the gauntlet of the other two partners.

And she wouldn't do it sitting in the car.

She glanced at her reflection in the mirror, dragging a comb through her thick dark hair. It swung neatly back into the bob, the ends curling obediently under, just grazing her shoulders. Her smoky green eyes, wide and incapable of deceit, stared unblinking back at her.

Just for courage, she winked at herself and her reflection winked cheekily back.

Here goes.

She got out of the car, locked it and strode confidently to the door.

The waiting-room was deserted, and the receptionist looked up with a smile. 'Can I help you?'

'Yes, I'm Emily Thompson. I'm here for an interview.'

The smile widened. 'Oh, hello, Dr Thompson. Dr Allen wasn't expecting you just yet—you can't have got lost.'

Emily laughed softly. 'Only a little. The directions were excellent.'

'I'm glad you thought so. I'm Sue Hooper, by the way—receptionist and general dogsbody. I'll tell Laurence you're here. Would you like to take a seat?'

'Thanks.'

She settled herself in one of the hard, upright chairs and looked around. Tiled floor—practical, but not very welcoming. Neat pile of magazines, but none of your glossies. *Farmer's Weekly*, *Woman's Weekly*, *My Weekly*, the odd *Reader's Digest*—a far cry from her last practice in Surrey.

There were pictures on the wall, faded and fly-blown, and the paint had seen better days, but the health-promotion posters and clinic details were fresh and up to date.

She glanced towards the door that must lead to the consulting-rooms, and saw an indicator board, with names and coloured lights, clearly used to call the next patient.

She scanned the names, and her heart came to an abrupt and grinding halt.

Dr D Trevellyan.

David.

Her mouth felt suddenly dry, and she flicked out her tongue and ran it over her lips. It couldn't be. Surely not? Trevellyan was a common enough Cornish name, and here, only forty miles or so from the Cornish border, it wouldn't be so very unusual.

And besides, the last she had heard of David he was working in London—probably destined for stardom as a Harley Street surgeon. God knows he had been a brilliant doctor even then, eight years ago. By now, with experience under his belt, he must be superb.

She glanced around the shabby, simple waiting-room. There was no way he would have to settle for this.

No, it couldn't be him. She hoped it wasn't, with all her heart, because quite apart from the fact that she wanted this job desperately for Jamie's sake she wasn't sure she could bear to see him again.

Sue came back, followed by a tall, stooping man with twinkling blue eyes and a welcoming smile.

'Dr Thompson—I'm sorry to keep you. You made very good time. I'm Laurence Allen.'

She rose to her feet, praying for calm, and returned his smile and handshake. 'You did specify an ability to map-read,' she reminded him.

He laughed. 'Yes—Robin's idea. The roads are a bit

like that, and the practice is very widespread. Come on through and meet him. I'm afraid David's not here at the moment, but he shouldn't be long. He had to go out on a call, but there'll be plenty of time to meet him.'

David. Oh, God, no, it couldn't be. . .

'Right, you'll do, Joe. Take it steady, give yourself time to get over this before you get back out there.'

The old man's wife gave a wheezy laugh. 'Might as well save your breath, Doctor—you know well as I do soon's your back's turned he'll be out there on the hills again.'

'Just give him the antibiotics and make sure he takes them regularly, Mrs Hardwill. Nothing you can do to help those that won't help themselves, eh, Joe?' David fixed the old man with his best steely glare. 'You help me, and I'll help you. I can't fix you without co-operation.'

Joe's racking cough filled the dingy, smoky room. He reached for a cigarette and David calmly removed them from him and put them on the mantelpiece.

'No—absolutely not.'

'Evil bugger, you are.'

'And I love you, too,' David said affectionately. 'Just be sensible, eh? Give your lungs a day or two to shake off this latest bout of bronchitis before you start poisoning them again.'

'Cough worse without,' he grumbled.

'Yes—because all the little hairs inside your tubes come back to life and start trying to sweep the rubbish out of your lungs——'

'Little hairs—load of old——'

David tutted and shook his head. 'Some people just don't want to be helped.' He snapped his bag shut and straightened up. 'Right, I have to get back; we're interviewing for the new partner.'

'Woman again?'

He nodded. 'Hope so.'

'Why any sane woman'd want to live in this God-forsaken part of the world beats me,' Mrs Hardwill said. 'Bain't nothin' here—no shoppin', no dancin'—or is she old, this one?'

'My age.'

'Spring chicken, then—bit of love interest, eh?' Joe ribbed wheezily.

David smiled dutifully. 'I doubt it, Joe. Don't hold your breath. Anyway, she's only recently widowed—and that's if we even appoint her. She's one of several we've seen. Now, remember, no smoking for a couple of days at least.'

He left the house to the sound of Joe's hacking cough, followed by his voice, wheezy and cracked, demanding his cigarettes.

'Damn quack—give me them down, woman.'

'No, I shan't, Joe Hardwill. You heard the doctor. . .'

He smiled and pulled the door to, and climbed back into his car.

Love interest, he thought as he headed back to the health centre. That was a joke. Since the disastrous demise of his marriage there had been no 'love interest'. One or two abortive attempts at rebuilding his life, but no relationship that offered any permanence or hope for the future.

No, there was only one woman—had only ever been one—and like a bloody fool he'd sent her away.

As he turned into the car park he noticed a strange car, and the number-plate had the name of a Surrey dealership on it.

So, the interviewee had made it. Their merry widow, as Laurence called her. Dr Emily Thompson. Even the name hurt him, he thought. Emily. Not his Emily, of course, but the name dragged up so many thoughts and feelings. Night after night he woke reaching for her, only to find his arms empty—as empty as his heart. Emily. . .

He squared his shoulders, threw a slightly off-centre smile at Sue and headed for the common-room. The sound of masculine laughter drifted to him down the corridor.

The interview was obviously going well. Thank God for that, because the other candidates had been decidedly weak. He could always call her Dr Thompson if he found the name too much.

He pushed the door open, and froze on the threshold. His heart crashed against his ribs, his mouth felt filled with cotton wool. From somewhere far away, he dredged up his voice.

'Emily. . .'

Like an old movie, frame by frame, heartbeat by heartbeat, she lifted her head and met his eyes.

'David. . .'

His name was a prayer on parched lips, and her eyes drank in her first sight of him in eight long, lonely years.

He hadn't changed at all—not in ways that mattered.

His hair, thick and dark, like polished mahogany, tousled by his impatient fingers, as always threatening to fall across those same incredible, clear grey eyes, the colour of morning mist; that full, sensuous mouth that had known her so intimately; the broad, square set of his shoulders set off by the soft lovat-green of his sports coat; the deep bottle-green polo neck that hugged his solid chest and smoothed over the flat, taut abdomen above lean, narrow hips and long, straight legs in well-cut cavalry twill; feet planted squarely on the floor, the tan brogues well-polished but worn and comfortable.

Only the smile was missing, and she found her own had gone the same way, together with her voice.

In silence she stared at him, absorbing the wonder of seeing him again at the same time as she registered regret, because now this job couldn't be hers, working with these wonderful, warm, friendly people in this beautiful part of the world.

'You two know each other, I take it?' Laurence said into the stretching silence.

Emily opened her mouth, but no sound emerged. She looked pleadingly at David.

'You could say that,' he murmured. 'We were married for five years.'

'Ah. . .'

Robin rose to his feet first. 'Um, Laurence, why don't we give these two a few minutes together?'

'Good idea.' Laurence scraped back his chair and stood up. 'We'll be in my office, David.'

David nodded. 'Fine. Thanks.'

The door closed softly behind them, but the two

hardly noticed. Their eyes were locked, trapped like flies in amber, unable to escape.

Then finally David dragged his eyes away and moved across the room, freeing her.

'Is the coffee still hot?'

His voice sounded strained—as well it might. Eight years was a long time.

'I think so,' she replied, and was amazed at the normality of her voice. Her greedy eyes sought out every tiny detail of his movements as he reached for the coffee-pot. Were his shoulders just a touch broader? Maybe. 'You're looking well,' she added.

He turned towards her, pot in hand. 'So are you—as lovely as ever.' His eyes flicked away. 'You got married again, I gather. I'm sorry to hear you lost your husband.'

Emily thought of Philip, one of the kindest, most generous men she had ever known, and felt a wash of sadness. 'Thank you,' she said quietly.

'You've got a son.' His voice sounded harsh, accusing almost. She ignored it.

'Yes—James. He's six now.'

'Rather young for you to have a full-time job.'

'I have to live,' she said, still quiet but defensive now.

'Yes—I'm sorry, your child-care arrangements are nothing to do with me.' He sat down in one of the easy-chairs, big hand wrapped round the mug of coffee, and eyed her over the top. 'So, what do you think of the practice?'

She shrugged. 'Wonderful. I would have loved working here, I'm sure.'

'Would have?'

She lifted her shoulders again. 'Of course. This changes things, don't you think?'

David was silent, regarding her through veiled eyes. She wished she could read his expression, but, like his looks, that aspect hadn't changed. She could never read his eyes if he didn't want her to.

The silence stretched on endlessly, and then finally he spoke. 'It needn't change things—not necessarily. We need a woman partner, and you were definitely the favoured candidate. We're very pushed, and we have been for some time. We need to make an appointment as soon as possible, really. Locums are difficult to come by. In this part of the world they want to work in Exeter or Barnstaple, not sleepy little Biddlecombe.'

His eyes traced her features one by one, then flicked back to lock with hers, their expression still unreadable. 'As for us—well, after all, it's been eight years. We should be able to be civilised about it.'

She thought of all the rows, and then of the making up, the desperate depths of passion he had aroused in her. Civilised? Somehow, knowing him, she doubted it.

She glanced around at the tired decorations. 'I wouldn't have thought this was your thing. I had you pegged for Harley Street.'

He gave a rude snort. 'Me? With my rural background and Cornish accent? I wouldn't smell right— that faint tang of manure that's so difficult to shift. Besides, I like it here.'

Her shoulders twitched. 'I just thought—you were such a brilliant doctor. I never expected you to bury yourself in obscurity.'

'Too good for general practice?' He snorted again.

'Was that why you went in for it? Because you weren't good enough for hospital medicine?'

Her head came up. 'How dare you? I am a good doctor——'

'So why bury yourself in obscurity?'

Their eyes clashed for a long while, and then a slow, lazy smile curved his lips. 'My round, I think,' he murmured, and his voice curled round her senses and sent a dart of something forgotten stabbing through her body.

She scraped up her ragged defences. 'I don't think this will work,' she said stiffly. 'We're fighting already.'

'Hardly fighting,' he countered, and she could see from his eyes that he was remembering—remembering the fights, and then the long, slow hours of making up. Sometimes she had wondered if they hadn't provoked half the fights just for the making up.

The pause stretched on. 'Give it a try, Emily,' he coaxed at last. 'If the others agree, give us six months— a probationary period. We would have had one anyway, whoever the candidate. See how it goes. If it really doesn't work, then fair enough, but give us a chance.'

Us? she thought. Which us? Us, the practice—or us, you and me, David and Emily, one-time lovers and best friends, with the stormiest marriage on record behind us? And a chance for what? To prove we can work together—or a chance to try again, to breathe life into the corpse of our long-buried love?

'I don't know,' she said quietly. 'I'm not sure I'm strong enough to handle it.'

'There's nothing to handle, Emily. Eight years is a

long time. We've changed, grown up, matured. We can deal with this.'

She looked at him, but he was staring out of the window and wouldn't meet her eyes.

Did he still feel anything for her? Possibly. Nostalgia? Fondness? Unlikely, considering the vitriolic row they had had before she walked out.

She could hide behind her widowhood, and Jamie — dear, sweet Jamie, so battered already by his short life. Nothing must hurt him now.

'I won't have an affair with you,' she said, hating to bring it up but needing to make the ground rules clear before they went any further.

He turned towards her then and met her eyes with a level stare. 'Did I suggest it?'

'No — but if you intended to the answer's no.'

His smile was slow and did terrifying things to her heart.

'I'll bear that in mind,' he said softly, and opened the door. 'Shall we go and have a word with the others?'

'They haven't said they want me yet,' she cautioned him.

He grinned, catching her off guard again with the boyish quirk of his lips.

'They want you — and so do I.'

The smoky glitter in his eyes made her heart race. 'David——'

'As a partner,' he added softly.

'No affair,' she reminded him, conscious of the ambiguity of his last remark.

'You've already mentioned that,' he said.

It was only later she realised he hadn't agreed to co-operate—and by then it was too late, because she'd agreed to take the job.

David spent the rest of that day wondering if he needed to have his bumps felt. He must have been nuts to suggest she take the job—just when the nights had begun to seem less long, when his career was on track and his life was ordered and tolerable.

He gave a bitter grunt of laughter. Tolerable? Who was he trying to kid? Emotionally it was a wasteland, a desert crying out for the sweet rain of her love, but would letting her back into his life be anything other than a mirage on the horizon, taunting him with the promise of long, cosy winter evenings by the fireside, followed by slow, lazy nights filled with passion and tenderness?

He dragged his thoughts to a halt, cursing softly as his body throbbed readily to life. Damn her. Damn her for coming back into his life. Damn the coincidence that had brought her back—and damn her for being so shatteringly, sweetly beautiful. All age had added was a soft, womanly maturity. There was no sign of the ravages of childbirth—at least none he could detect, and despite his better intentions he had looked hard enough.

No, she was still his Emily, the woman who had haunted his days and nights for the past eight years, the woman who had taken away his future and left him with nothing but bittersweet memories of a less than perfect past.

He stared out of his surgery window at the hillside opposite, the rolling folds of the valley that fell steadily to the sea two miles away.

It was a beautiful place to live, a place to find peace and tranquillity, if not happiness—until Emily.

Except, if he had to be honest, he had come here initially because of her, or at least because of those accursed memories.

They had spent two blissful, glorious weeks here on their honeymoon, courtesy of Emily's old schoolfriend Sarah, whose parents had owned a cottage not five miles away—a cottage where they had both given up their virginity in a fumbling, earth-shattering explosion of tension—at least his tension had exploded then. Emily's explosion had been a little later, when he had blundered his way towards a better understanding of her body and its responses, but when he had. . .

Remembering those responses drew a deep, agonised groan from him now, and he dropped his head into his hands, knuckling his eyes and forcing his breath through a chest that felt as if a steel band was coiled tightly round it.

Need—years of aching, unsatisfied need—rose up to swamp him. The dull, heavy throb of his body taunted him, and every time his eyes flickered shut she danced naked against his lids as she had in the cottage that bleak December of their honeymoon, her smooth skin lit only by the dancing flames of the fire.

He groaned again and stood up, only to sit down again and force his attention to the demands of paperwork until the embarrassing and unmistakable hunger in his body subsided.

Damn her.

And damn him for stopping her when she had wanted to go away earlier today and forget all about this job.

He should have let her go while the going was good.
Idiot.

It was no good, he was never going to get this
paperwork done today. What he needed was some
fresh air. There was a patient he needed to visit, too—
he'd go and do it and take his mind off his folly, at
least for a little while.

The door creaked open, cobwebs clinging to the frame,
and Emily stepped cautiously over the threshold. It
smelt musty, but it seemed dry enough. She walked
hestitantly into the sitting-room and faltered to a
standstill.

It hadn't changed—not since—oh, lord.

Memories came back to swamp her—David, lying
naked on the hearthrug, watching her hungrily as she
danced in front of the flames, his eyes warming her
pale skin as effectively as the fire. He had reached for
her, drawing her down beside him, then his body had
claimed hers again——

She became conscious of a dull, heavy ache of need,
buried long ago deep down inside her, and the slow,
insistent beat of her heart beneath her breasts.

She must be mad, she thought with a moan as she
pressed cool palms against her flaming cheeks. Mad to
think she could come back here to live, in this cottage
which held so many memories. And madder still to
think she could work side by side with the man who
had helped to make those memories.

Her eyes strayed back to the fire, and, sinking down
on to the hearthrug, she let her fingers stray over the
soft woollen pile.

He had been so tender with her, so nervous himself and yet so thoughtful of her. . .

'Isn't it lovely?'

David glanced round, then back to his bride, her cheeks glowing with health and something else.

'Absolutely,' he said huskily, but she knew he wasn't talking about the cottage and her throat went dry.

Her whole body tingled with anticipation, with the tension that had built between them until now.

But it would end here, tonight, their wedding night.

'It's cold,' he murmured. 'I'll light the fire.'

It was reluctant, and she laughed at him and pushed him out of the way, interfering.

In the end, amid much teasing and hilarity, they got it going, and David went out to the car and brought in the luggage and a bottle of champagne.

The fridge, they found, was full of goodies courtesy of Sarah's parents—the lady who looked after the cottage had been in and cleaned it, made up the beds and stocked up with groceries at their instruction.

'How kind,' Emily said to David, and he agreed and turned to her.

'What about supper?'

'I'm not really hungry,' she confessed, her eyes tangling with his.

'No, nor am I. Shall we sit by the fire and open the champagne?'

They found glasses and settled down on the hearth-rug. Although the heating was on it was a cold, cheerless day and darkness had fallen some time before. There, though, in the flickering firelight, the outside world was forgotten.

'To us,' he said softly, touching his glass to hers, and, their eyes locked, they entwined their arms and sipped deeply.

She wrinkled her nose. 'Bubbles,' she said, a little breathless, and he leaned back against a chair and pulled her between his legs, her back against his chest, one arm resting comfortably across her waist.

Her head was tipped back against his throat, and she could feel the beat of his heart against her shoulders.

'It was a lovely day, wasn't it?' she said softly.

'I thought it would never end,' he murmured.

She turned her head a little and stared up at him. The flames were reflected in his eyes, but then he moved his head and she saw a fire in them that was all his own. She swallowed, her heart suddenly pounding, and he took her glass away and set it down with his.

Then he reached for her, a little clumsily, and she turned in his arms to meet his kiss. Their passion caught and blazed, yet he seemed reluctant somehow, as if he was holding back.

She lifted her head and looked at him. 'What's wrong?'

He shook his head slightly. 'I so badly want this to be special for you, but I expect it's going to be a disaster,' he confessed, his voice trembling a little. 'I've never done it before, so don't expect miracles.'

She reached up and cupped his cheek. 'Nor have I, so don't worry. I don't know what to expect—except that it might hurt.'

His eyes clouded. 'I don't want to hurt you, Emily.'

'Well, we can't wait forever,' she told him with typical candour. 'I suppose it will only be the once.'

'I'll be as gentle as I can.'

'I know.'

He reached out his arms again and kissed her once more, slowly, softly, with all his love—or so it seemed, because suddenly Emily found she didn't care how much it hurt, she just needed to hold him and be held by him, to feel his body on hers, to know him in the oldest sense.

She reached for his shirt buttons, freeing two and sliding her fingers inside against the warm, smooth skin. A light scatter of hair grazed her knuckles, sending shivers down her spine.

'Cold?' he asked, but she shook her head.

'No—no, not cold.'

He moved away a little from her, and stripped off his jacket and tie, then his shirt.

Her heart thudded and crashed against her ribs. He was so—male? She felt liquid heat pooling low down, just where her body ached for him. She couldn't drag her eyes from him, and as he slid his trousers down the taut, well-muscled thighs she thought she would die of wanting him.

He turned back to her, his scanty briefs doing little to hide his need for her, and she flicked her tongue out and moistened her dry lips.

'Your turn,' he said gruffly, and helped her to her feet.

'You do it,' she whispered.

'I don't know where to start——'

'Zip at the back,' she told him, and, turning round, she lifted her hair and bent her head forward.

She felt the slide of the zip, then the warmth of his lips pressed against her spine.

'You smell wonderful,' he breathed against her skin, and a shiver ran over her.

Turning in his arms, she slipped the dress down over her shoulders and stepped out of it.

The breath left him as if he'd been punched. He lifted trembling hands and curved them lightly over her barely covered breasts.

'Emily,' he whispered raggedly, and she arched into his hands, pressing her aching breasts against his palms. His fingers tightened convulsively as her hands locked behind him and drew them together, then as their hips brushed against each other they both gasped.

'I need you,' he said, the words shattering against her cheek.

'I'm yours,' she said simply, her shyness forgotten.

He drew her down on the rug and slowly, his hands shaking, he stripped away the scraps of silk and lace that hid her from his eyes.

'Emily,' he breathed.

She'd thought she would feel shy, but the awestruck reverence of his expression dispelled her last fears. Slipping her fingers in the waistband of his briefs, she eased them down and abandoned them, turning back to study his now totally naked form.

He took her breath away.

'Let me touch you,' he murmured, and she lay down again beside him, her hands reaching for his shoulders, smoothing the hot satin of his skin.

Tremblingly, his hands traced her body, cupping her breasts, gliding over the sleek skin of her flank, his knuckles grazing her inner thighs. Her legs fell open for him, her hips arching up against his hand as he straightened his fingers and laid his palm against the damp nest of curls.

Her own caresses grew braver, her hands sliding down his sides, her fingers curling round him, hot satin over steel.

His breath caught and he dropped his head against her shoulder.

'Steady,' he muttered.

She could feel the moisture pooling as he stroked her, feel the tension rising even higher. She didn't want to be steady. She wanted to be his.

'Oh, David, now,' she moaned.

Her breath was choking her, her heart thrashing against her ribs as he moved awkwardly over her.

'Help me,' he pleaded, and just as awkwardly she did as he asked, guiding him towards the heavy ache inside her.

'I love you,' he said against her mouth, and there was a brief flash of pain and then fullness—fullness that she had never even dreamt of. . .

'Are you OK?' he asked, his voice taut.

'Oh, yes—oh, David. . .'

Her hands gripped his shoulders and she strained up against him, unable to bear the tension. 'Oh, David, please, do something. . .'

'Oh, Emily—oh, God, I. . .'

His body started to move, winding the tension higher, and then suddenly he stiffened, dropping his head into the curve of her shoulder, his harsh cry muffled against her skin.

Then he collapsed, his body trembling under her hands, his chest heaving.

She lay there, her hands smoothing him, and slow tears slipped from her eyes.

She needed more—her body screamed for more, for some elusive release that only David had found.

He lifted his head. 'I'm sorry—oh, Emily, you're crying. I did hurt you.'

'No—no, you didn't. It's just. . .' She hesitated, unable to voice her need, but it was unnecessary.

Shifting slightly, he slid his hand between them and touched her. 'Is that right?' he asked softly. 'Tell me.'

She was beyond speech, beyond anything but the feel of his hand touching, soothing, yet winding the tension even higher until——

'David!' she sobbed, and, burying her face against his shoulder, she felt the ripples spreading, lifting her higher, higher, until suddenly she was over the crest and there before her was paradise. . .

They came slowly back to earth, their arms wrapped tightly round each other, their legs still tangled, and David rained tiny, butterfly-kisses over her face.

'Are you OK?' he murmured softly.

'Mmm. You?'

Shyly, she met his eyes, and nearly melted at the love in them.

He was speechless, just hugging her closer. 'You were wonderful,' he said eventually. 'I had no idea it would feel so—oh, Em. . .'

'Nor did I,' she whispered, thinking of that unbelievable fullness, the rightness of his body joined with hers.

'Next time I'll wait for you,' he vowed.

They grew cold, and while David explored the fridge she unpacked her dressing-gown and had a shower.

By the time she went back down he was dressed

again in jeans and a sweatshirt, and had put some salad out on plates.

'We've got champagne to finish,' he told her, and they sat together on the hearthrug and fed each other nibbles of salad and toasted their toes in front of the blazing logs until the champagne was finished.

David had put on some music, and, emboldened by the champagne and the look in his eyes, she stood up, swaying softly to the music.

'Dance with me,' she said.

He shook his head. 'Dance for me,' he murmured.

So she did, slipping the dressing-gown over her shoulders to puddle on the floor, teasing and taunting until with a ragged groan he drew her down before the fire and made love to her again. . .

'Emily?'

She turned, startled, to find David framed in the doorway.

Her first thought was that he wasn't naked. Her second was that her memories must be written all across her face in letters ten feet high.

She felt colour rush to her cheeks and was grateful for the gloomy light in the room.

'Why are you here?' she asked breathlessly.

'I was just passing and I saw your car,' he told her. His eyes were on the fireplace, then flicked back to her kneeling on the hearthrug where they had made love that very first time. Something flickered in his eyes, and she could tell he was remembering, too.

She struggled to her feet.

'I was just having a look.'

He glanced round. 'For old times' sake? It hasn't changed,' he said softly.

Their eyes met, clashed, locked. Her breath clogged her throat, her heart beating a wild tattoo against her ribs.

'No,' she murmured.

'No, what?' he asked, his voice husky.

'No, not for old times' sake,' she said, firming her voice. 'I'm going to be living here.'

'Oh.' His eyes travelled slowly over her, so that she was conscious of her nipples straining against the fine fabric of her blouse. His eyes strayed lower, then jerked back to her face with an almost physical effort. 'Good idea,' he said, his voice still touched with that smoky gruffness she remembered so well from the intimate moments of their marriage. 'It's very handy for the practice—is Sarah renting it to you?' he asked.

She dropped her eyes. 'No—she's—Sarah died two years ago. She left me the cottage.'

'Oh, Emily—I'm sorry. What happened?'

His voice had changed instantly, softening with compassion, and she swallowed the lump in her throat as she thought back to the awful night when Sarah had died.

'A car accident,' she told him hollowly. 'It was foggy. A drunk driver——'

David groaned. 'What a waste. Oh, my love, I'm sorry.'

So was Emily, because she hadn't wanted Sarah to drive in the fog. 'Stay,' she had begged her, but she should have been more insistent, hidden her keys or something. Sarah had been upset, too, too upset to drive really, because that was the day she had found out that Philip was dying of cancer—Philip, her beloved husband, Jamie's father—and the man Emily had then married so that her godson's future would be secure.

CHAPTER TWO

EMILY arrived to take up her post two weeks later, having sent the housekeeper on ahead to clean up the cottage and prepare it for her arrival with Jamie.

He was thoughtful about leaving the big house in Surrey where he had lived with his parents, but she explained that they wouldn't be selling it yet and could always come back for visits. Anyway, she remembered how much Jamie had wanted to move to Devon, how he had begged her. That was one reason, probably the most significant, why she had taken the job. She just hoped for all their sakes that it didn't prove a huge mistake.

'Are we going to live in Mummy's cottage, Emmy?' he asked for the hundredth time on the drive down. He was so insecure now, and she hastened to reassure him.

'Yes, darling. We'll be there tonight.'

'Will I have my own room?'

'Yes, of course.'

There was the question of where she would sleep, but as the cottage had four bedrooms there was no need for her to use the room that Sarah and Philip had used—and that she had slept in with David on their honeymoon.

Mrs Bradley, the housekeeper who had been with Philip's family for years and who was to stay on to help care for Jamie at Philip's behest, would have the large room next to Jamie as her bed-sitting room. Emily would have the fourth bedroom.

It was small, but she was on her own, so it didn't matter. Anyway, it had a distant view of the sea down the valley and across the rooftops of Biddlecombe, and the sun would wake her every morning.

They arrived at the cottage to a warm welcome from Mrs Bradley, and within a very short time Jamie was settled in his bed, his teddy under his arm, his thumb tucked in his mouth, and Emily was sitting down with Mrs Bradley going over the arrangements for the beginning of the next week when Emily started work and Jamie would join the village school. She had managed to get a place for him, and the headmaster was looking forward to meeting the boy on Monday.

The only thing left to concern her was David, and the prospect of working with him made the ergonomics of her accommodation and Jamie's schooling pale into insignificance.

In fact her first morning at the surgery was much easier than she had expected, because he greeted her with a friendly smile, gave her a cup of coffee and took himself off, leaving it to Laurence to make her feel at home and show her where everything was kept.

Her first patients were genuinely in need, but she had no doubt that after a few days word would get round and she would be inundated with people giving their noses a treat.

Her clinics, she noticed, were already booked some way ahead, especially the family planning and antenatal.

'They like a woman for a woman's domain,' Sue said with a smile. 'I have to agree—but if you feel you've got too many I can shift some back to David, although he won't like it. Some of them flirt with him, but you can't blame them. He's just such a sexy beast——Oh, lord, I'm sorry!' Her hand flew over her mouth, and Emily smiled at her discomfort.

'Sue, forget it. It was ages ago, and I'm over him,' she lied. 'Don't feel you have to walk on eggshells, please. One thing, though—I'd rather the patients didn't know we'd been married.'

'Oh, of course not,' Sue agreed. 'It's nobody's business but your own, and I'm sorry I said what I did.'

Emily smiled again. 'You're right, though—he is a sexy beast.'

'You couldn't be talking about me, could you?'

David's voice behind made her jump, and she turned towards him with a cool smile. 'Your ego's still intact, I see. No, we were talking about Robert de Niro, actually. Excuse me.'

She slipped past him and retreated to her office, closing the door behind her.

It opened almost immediately.

'Can I have a word?'

She shrugged. She couldn't shut him out of her life completely; they had to work together.

'Of course.'

She waved to a seat and positioned herself safely behind her desk. 'What can I do for you?'

He sighed thoughtfully. 'Oh, Emily, there's a question and a half.'

'David. . .' Her voice contained a warning, and he grinned, melting her insides.

She almost groaned aloud. Sue was right—he was a sexy beast.

'This afternoon,' he said, the grin replaced by a businesslike expression that wasn't nearly so heart-melting—thank God, she thought. He went on, 'Mr and Mrs Blake are coming to see you. They're my patients, and I don't know what they want—perhaps it's family planning or something. Anyway, they specifically requested an appointment with the new lady doctor when she arrived, and the appointment's been booked for over a week.'

'I'll tell you what it's about,' she promised.

He nodded. 'OK. I'll be around if you want to refer to me—perhaps sneak out to get a form from reception or some such excuse.'

She eyed him curiously. 'Do you really think that'll be necessary?'

He shrugged. 'Probably not. I just get a feeling about them. I don't think they're all that happy together, and a joint appointment with a stranger——' He shrugged again. 'Could be nothing, of course, but I just thought I'd prime you. Right.'

He unfolded his legs and stretched his hands over his head, yawning widely. 'Oh, God, I hate weekends on duty. I'm going home to walk the dogs—I'll be back before two for my clinic. What are you doing about lunch?'

She opened her drawer and pulled out some sandwiches.

'You don't want to come with me and grab a snack at home and a quick stroll over the hill?'

It sounded lovely, just the way they had spent their honeymoon, but she forced herself to shake her head. This was hardly the way to start, and working with him would be hard enough without encouraging little intimate walks over the hills.

'I think not,' she said as firmly as she could manage, and with a rueful grin he left her alone, wondering if she'd lost her marbles completely or if it just seemed that way.

She should have known to trust his instincts, she thought as she studied the couple opposite her.

They were in their thirties, a very average professional couple, but the way the consultation was going was far from average.

'Of course,' Mr Blake was saying, 'we'd probably stand more chance of having another child if the first one wasn't always in our bed.'

Mrs Blake's eyes slid away, and Emily's own instincts prickled. Her attention switched to the woman.

'How old is your child?'

'Four—and she has terrible nightmares. If we don't have her in bed with us, she wakes screaming and it takes ages to settle her down again.'

'Not that long,' her husband argued.

'No, well, it isn't you that ends up doing it,' she returned bitterly. 'You just lie there on your back snoring your head off and complain that I've woken you with the creaky boards—though if you'd ever put them down again properly after you fixed that pipe they wouldn't creak——'

'I think we're rather getting off the point,' Emily interjected gently but firmly. 'I have a son of six, and when his father died recently he was very upset. He started getting into bed with me at night, and I could see this becoming a pattern, so what I did was when he woke I got into his bed for a little while and gave him a cuddle, then slipped out again when he'd gone off. If he came to me, I'd carry him back once he'd settled.'

She regarded the couple in front of her. 'It worked for us—it might work for you. I certainly don't think you can leave a child upset in the middle of the night, but to allow her presence to affect your relationship to this extent I think is probably not healthy either for the child or for you——'

'Not healthy?' Mr Blake bristled. 'Are you accusing us of abusing her or something?'

'No, of course not,' Emily soothed. 'I'm simply suggesting that a better sleep-pattern, undisturbed by a frightened child, or more opportunities to concentrate on the physical aspect of your relationship might be emotionally and physically healthier for all of you.'

'Well, it wasn't my idea to have her in bed with us in the first place, and she's much worse now than she used to be.'

'And I suppose that's my fault!' Mrs Blake said defensively—too defensively.

Clearly, Emily thought, she wasn't going to get anywhere until she split these two up—and perhaps a word with the intuitive Dr Trevellyan might be in order.

'I don't seem to have all your notes here,' she said blandly to them. 'If you'll excuse me a moment, I'll just go and see what I can find in the office.'

She nipped out of the door and down the corridor. Sue was on the reception desk, and Emily asked if she knew where David was.

'In his office—he's alone, so if you want to go in you can. I think he's half expecting you.'

She knocked on the door and went in. 'You were right,' she said directly.

'The Blakes? What's the problem?'

'He's complaining that they can't have another child because the first is still coming into their bed at night and so they don't have the opportunity. Reading between the lines, I would say Mrs Blake isn't keen anyway. Apparently they've been trying for over a year.'

David's eyebrows shot up. 'Have they, indeed? So why did she come and see me six months ago for another diaphragm?'

Emily's jaw dropped, and then she nodded. 'Oh, that figures. The child's a smokescreen—she's using her so she doesn't have to sleep with her husband—or, at least, can only sleep.'

'Hmm.'

'Hmm?'

'I heard a rumour—it might be nothing, but she could be having an affair.'

Emily's mouth formed a round O. 'Tricky.'

'Very. I'll give you the details later. Split them up, send him in to me for a physical, and get her to spill the beans.'

'OK. Now?'

'Yeah, send him straight in. I'll return him to the waiting-room.'

She went back and sent Mr Blake to David, then confronted Mrs Blake.

'OK. On your notes it says you have a diaphragm. I've spoken to Dr Trevellyan; he confirmed it.'

Panic flared in the woman's eyes. 'He won't tell Neil, will he? I mean, it is confidential?'

'Of course he won't tell him. And clearly you haven't, or else you wouldn't be here today talking about infertility.'

She let the silence stretch, then Mrs Blake gave a shaky sigh and reluctantly met Emily's eyes. 'I don't want another baby,' she said slowly. 'At least, not Neil's.'

'Things don't seem all sweetness and light between you,' Emily acknowledged.

The woman gave a short, bitter laugh. 'You could say that. It was OK for a while, we struggled along making the best of it, but then—there's someone else, someone I love——' She pressed her fingers to her mouth, clearly upset, and Emily settled back in the chair.

'Take your time,' she said reassuringly.

'He's wonderful—warm, tender, understanding.' She paused. 'He's also married.'

'Ah.'

'His wife's disabled. He loves her, but like a sister, you know? Not that there could be anything else between them. She's got multiple sclerosis, and she's—well, she's bad.'

'Oh, dear.' Emily's soft heart went out to the unknown woman whose husband apparently loved her, but not enough to stay at home.

'She's permanently bedridden now—she's incontinent and her limbs are very spastic. She finds swallowing difficult, and she's very depressed.' Ann Blake looked at Emily. 'I'd hate her to find out about us, but Richard's coping all alone and someone has to help him through it. He gives her so much, not just his time but friendship, support—he gets really depressed. That was how it started, really—he was sitting in the park, and I was out with Jane and the dog. He looked so bleak, so alone. We started to talk, and. . .'

Ann paused, her face softening. 'He laughed, for the first time in months, he said. I saw him again by accident, and then we began arranging to meet, always quite innocently. We never meant this to happen.'

'But it did.'

'Yes. And all I want is to be with him, but I can't.'

'And meanwhile you're living with a man you no longer love, who wants to have another child.'

She nodded, and her eyes filled. 'What can I do? Richard can't leave Jenny, and I can't afford to leave Neil and live on my own with Jane. Anyway, he'd probably want custody and she loves him.'

'Is it fair to her to use her as a smokescreen?'

There was silence for a long while, then Mrs Blake shook her head. 'No—no, of course not. I didn't even realise I was doing it until just now. It was only when you suggested that if we put her back in her own bed it would give our physical relationship a chance that I realised how badly I didn't want that to happen.'

Emily eyed her thoughtfully. 'Mrs Blake, when did you and your husband last make love?'

She snorted. 'We don't make love, Dr Thompson. We had sex back in—June? July? And that was the first time since Easter.'

'And it's now September. How long can you fool him?'

She shrugged helplessly. 'I don't know.'

'Nor do I,' Emily told her, 'but one thing I do know—it isn't fair to Jane to use her like this. She must start sleeping in her own bed again, and I don't mean with you. How you persuade your husband that you aren't going to have intercourse is your problem, but if you want any help or counselling advice you can always go to Relate, the marriage guidance people. They're very good. Perhaps you ought to try it.'

'And what can they do?' Ann asked heavily. 'Make me fall back in love with Neil again? I doubt it.'

So did Emily, but there was nothing more she could do. There was clearly no fertility problem that exposure to the appropriate opportunity wouldn't solve, and there was obviously no need for any further medical involvement. How Mrs Blake dealt with it from here was her own problem, and it was one Emily didn't envy her one bit.

As she was leaving, she turned back to Emily. 'Dr Thompson, this is confidential, isn't it? I mean, whatever we've told each other in here won't get back to Neil?'

'No, of course not. Not without your permission.'

'So he won't ever know what went on in here today?'

As Emily confirmed that, it occurred to her that it was a strange way to phrase the question. After her surgery was over she went and sought David out.

'Tricky one,' he said. 'I expect she intends to lie through her teeth to him.'

'Oh, dear. Do you think he'll come back for some answers?'

David shrugged. 'Depends how convincing she is. Some women aren't very convincing liars.'

He was looking at her oddly, as if he was referring to her, and she felt her heart thud uncomfortably. Not that she had lied—except by omission, to allow him to think that Jamie was hers.

Still, his eyes searched hers as he stood up and came slowly round the end of the desk.

'I ought to tell you all about the man she's having the affair with. Why don't we do it over a drink on the way home?'

She had to physically stop herself from backing up against the wall to get away from him.

'No! I mean—I'm tired, and it was Jamie's first day at school. I ought to get back and see him and ask Mrs Bradley how he was when she picked him up.'

'Mrs Bradley?'

'Our housekeeper.'

David's brows quirked slightly. 'Housekeeper, eh? I thought you'd have an au pair.'

Emily shook her head. 'No—it was a provision of Philip's will that she have a home with us for life, and a living allowance. He left us all very well provided for, and Mrs Bradley's just another example of his thoughtfulness. She's been with his family for years, and Jamie knows her. It seemed very sensible, and to be honest I'm very grateful to her for all she does. I couldn't do my job properly without her.'

'No, I can see that,' he said. He paused, those soft grey eyes searching her face until the need to run was paramount. And yet he wasn't threatening—rather the reverse. His hand came up and brushed a stray lock of hair away from her face, and she quivered at his touch. 'Poor Emily,' he said softly. 'It must be very hard for you. How does Jamie cope with his mother working when his father's died so recently?'

She should have corrected him then, but she didn't—another lost opportunity. Tonight, though, didn't seem to be the time. Instead she focused on his words. 'I

haven't worked since Philip became very ill near the
end.'

'Was it cancer?'

She nodded. 'Yes—stomach cancer. For ages he
thought he had an ulcer. By the time they realised it
wasn't, it was too late.'

'But you didn't pick it up?'

She shook her head. How could she have done? She
wasn't there; but David didn't know that. She must
find a time to tell him all that had happened, before he
thought she was deceiving him. After all they had been
through, she owed him honesty, even though Jamie
made a useful smokescreen.

To think she had just finished telling Ann Blake that
she couldn't use her daughter to hide behind!

And Jamie, her son or not, needed her now. She
might not be his mother, but she was the closest the
poor child would ever get, and she fully intended to do
her job well. 'I must get home,' she said now. 'Jamie
will be fretting.'

'Of course.'

He seemed suddenly distant, and for a moment
Emily felt a shocking sense of loss sweep through her.

Absurd.

Without giving herself time to think, she bade him
goodnight and made her way out.

He was the last person she would want to see, David
told himself disgustedly, but it didn't stop him pulling
up outside her cottage with a pot plant from the local
garage and a bottle of plonk.

It was only a welcome to the area, after all, a simple
gesture from an old friend.

And he might get to meet this child of hers, the child she had conceived not two years after their separation—before their divorce was final, even.

He fought down the bitter jealousy that surged in his veins, and concentrated instead on juggling the plant and bottle while he locked his car. Perhaps he should just go, he thought, take the stuff to the surgery in the morning and forget about invading her privacy——

'Can I help you?'

A matronly woman stood in the open doorway, lit from behind by the welcoming glow that spilt from the cottage across the path to his feet. It didn't quite reach him, and somehow stepping into the light suddenly assumed an almost mystical significance.

'Is Emily at home?' he asked, remaining where he was.

'Who should I say it is?' she responded, without inviting him in.

'David—David Trevellyan.'

The door was immediately held wider, and a smile broke out on the woman's face. 'Come in, Dr Trevellyan. I'll fetch her—she's putting Jamie to bed.'

He stepped into the light, his heart easing even as he did so. 'Could you find a home for these? Just a sort of housewarming present.'

'How kind.' The warm hazel eyes twinkled like currants above plump cheeks that rose with her smile and squashed her eyes into merry slits. David found himself returning the smile and feeling grateful that Emily and her son had such a kindly soul caring for them.

'Make yourself at home, Dr Trevellyan—I'll just pop these in the kitchen and go and find Emily.'

He stood in the hallway while she bustled into the kitchen and then out again, hurrying up the stairs.

He heard a mumbled conversation overhead, then Emily appeared at the top of the stairs.

'David?'

Was it his imagination, or did she sound breathless?

He tipped his head back and shielded his eyes from the overhead light. 'Hi. I just wondered if you wanted to go out for that drink now—if Jamie's settled.'

'Oh.' She looked flustered, her hands fluttering over her clothes. 'I'm not really dressed for going out.'

'That's OK. The local isn't smart; your jeans are fine.'

More than fine, if the tightening in his body was anything to go by.

'Um—let me brush my hair and I'll be down.'

He watched as she turned, the faded denim taut over the smooth curve of her bottom, and cursed softly under his breath.

He must be mad.

Emily felt sick with fright—or was it anticipation? Ridiculous. She brushed her hair until the roots protested, then dragged a scrape of colour over her lips and smudged them hastily together. That would do. It would have to.

Abandoning her brush, she ran down the stairs like an eager teenager.

'Ready?' he asked.

She nodded. 'I just need my coat.'

He held it for her, his fingers brushing her neck as he lifted her hair away from the collar in a gesture she remembered so well. A little shiver ran over her skin and, forcing a smile, she turned to him.

'Shall we?'

He opened the door for her, closed it behind them and then settled her into the car before going round and sliding behind the wheel.

The inside of the car seemed suddenly terribly small and intimate, and her breathing seemed unnaturally loud.

'Where are we going?' she asked to fill the emptiness.

'The Bull—remember it?'

She did—vividly. They had spent many a happy lunchtime there, sandwiched between long, lazy mornings in bed and long, equally lazy evenings in front of the fire at the cottage.

'Has it changed?'

'Not much. Nothing round here changes much. It gets a bit hectic in the summer, but at this time of year it's mainly locals.'

They pulled up in the nearly deserted car park, and she followed him through the low doorway into the heavily beamed lounge that was empty except for a grizzled, thick-set man wiping down the bar.

'Evening, George.'

'Evening, Doctor. What'll it be?'

'I'll have the usual—Emily?'

'Dry white wine, please.'

George set the drinks on the bar and eyed her curiously.

'This is Dr Thompson—she's just joined the practice,' David told him.

'Pleased to meet you—you'll cheer that place up no

end,' he said gruffly, and pushed a glass of wine towards her. 'Here—have them on the house.'

She smiled, his welcome warming her. 'Thank you. Cheers—your very good health.'

His rusty laugh crackled in the empty room. 'Of course, you've got a vested interest in that, haven't you? Keep the surgery empty.'

She smiled again. 'I don't think there's much chance of that. Still, at least you won't have to pretend to be ill to satisfy your curiosity.'

He laughed again as he headed for the other bar, and David steered her over to a table in the corner, tucked in behind the deep chimney breast where they had often sat during their honeymoon. It was too intimate, and she was very conscious of his nearness.

He lifted his glass, condensation beaded on the outside, fogging the pale beer. 'Here's to a long and happy partnership,' he murmured.

His eyes were in shadow, but she sensed the intensity of his gaze. Was he talking about the practice? Or them? She didn't dare ask.

She lifted her glass, dropping her eyes to the contents. Silently she drank, the chilled wine soothing her tight throat.

'So,' she said eventually, 'tell me about Ann Blake and this affair.'

'Ah.' He set his glass down precisely in the centre of a beermat and squared it up with the edge of the table. The task seemed to require an inordinate amount of attention.

'Richard Wellcome is a local farmer. He and his wife are patients of mine. His wife, Jenny, has MS and is in a pretty sorry way. She hasn't had much in the way of remission, and I don't think she will. She's getting increasingly spastic—she's on Baclofen to combat it, but it's a bit of a juggling act because it makes her very sleepy, and she keeps dropping things. Last week it was a cup of tea. Luckily it wasn't too hot or she could have had a nasty scald.'

'Poor woman.'

'Mmm. And Richard, of course, is having a hard time. The farm's not doing too well, and he's hiding the real situation from Jenny because he doesn't want to worry her. What with one thing and another, I'm not surprised he's having an affair.'

'Do you condone it?' Emily asked sharply.

He sighed. 'Don't be judgemental, Emily. Life's hard. We take what ease we can. If Ann helps him to cope, then so be it.'

'But her own marriage is in ruins as a result.'

'Her marriage has been in ruins for years. Women don't have affairs with other women's husbands if everything's rosy at home. She was ripe for the picking.'

'And that justifies it?'

He shrugged. 'Maybe.'

She felt anger stir her, an old, familiar anger remembered from their earlier fights. It shocked her, but she couldn't help responding to it.

'David, you can't just accept it like that. You should encourage her to seek help, to go to Relate and find a solution——'

'Why? I'm their doctor, not their priest.'

'But you should treat the whole person.'

'You're assuming that infidelity is an illness. You

can't interfere in people's lives, Emily. That's not what you're there for.'

'But what about the child?' she argued.

'What about her? They'll sort themselves out, one way or another.'

She let out her breath on a whoosh. 'I can't believe you're that callous.'

'I'm not callous,' he reasoned. 'I just know my limitations. Medically speaking, Richard Wellcome is the one with the need. He's a depressive—and if Ann Blake acts as an antidepressant that helps him through his life, then who am I to take her away from him? Besides, if he can cope, then Jenny can stay at home, which is what she wants. She was born there; technically it's her farm. Richard was employed by her father to work the farm once he became too ill to manage it any more. I think he feels that quite keenly.'

'And if it's going badly, that's quite a responsibility.'

'Exactly. It's a hell of a coil, Emily. You're better off having as little to do with it as possible.' He tipped back his head and drained his glass, his throat bobbing as he swallowed.

Emily watched, transfixed. He set the glass down. 'Another one?'

She shook her head. 'No, I don't think so. I ought to be getting back; I'm quite tired.'

'You've had a busy day,' he said softly, and, helping her into her coat again, he ushered her out of the door.

They were silent on the journey back, and when he pulled up outside her cottage she reached immediately for the handle.

Her mouth, however, was on his side.

'Coffee?' she found herself asking.

'In a minute.'

His hand on her shoulder turned her back towards him, and in the light from the porch she could see need glittering in his eyes.

She knew he was going to kiss her before he reached for her—before the warmth of his arms enfolded her against his chest, before the softness of his lips brushed against hers once, twice, before settling firmly against her mouth. One of them sighed, a ragged, broken sigh of remembrance, and then thoughts fled, lost in the heat that flared between them as their mouths met and melded, locked in a passion as old as time.

After an age he lifted his head and stared down at her, his eyes dark. 'You taste the same,' he whispered wonderingly.

'So do you.'

Her voice was fractured, scrapy. She eased away from him, needed room to order her thoughts.

'Coffee, I think,' he said, and his voice was ragged too.

She had forgotten her offer of coffee, but it was too late now to take it back.

They got out of the car and went in.

CHAPTER THREE

EMILY led him into the sitting-room, gleaming with polish and warmed by the flickering flames of the fire.

'It's a little early in the year, but I always think a fire's so cheerful, don't you?'

David's mind was hardly paying attention. The flickering firelight brought back so many memories. Fighting back the lump in his throat, he dredged up a smile. 'Absolutely,' he said. Damn, she looked so lovely, her lips lush and full, just kissed.

He shouldn't have done that, yet for the life of him he couldn't have stopped himself. In fact, if she didn't move away from him soon, he was going to do it again——

'I'll go up and check on Jamie,' she said, and backed away, her eyes wide.

She almost ran through the door, and his eyes tracked her departure, lingering on the smooth curve of her bottom, tightly clad in the jeans. His hands itched to cup the sleek swell, to grasp her hips and pull her hard against him, as if that would somehow ease the gnawing ache he felt for her.

Alone, he wandered round the room fingering her possessions. Some, like the little jade buddha, he remembered. Others were new, like the table smothered in photographs in old silver frames. There was one of her with Sarah taken in their teens, and another, also with Sarah and obviously at her wedding.

He studied them, needing the distraction, and found a photo of Sarah and her husband staring into each other's eyes, their love clearly visible. He felt a pang of sadness for her young life snuffed out in its prime. He had always liked Emily's old schoolfriend.

Another photo, this one of a christening, with Emily holding a baby and Sarah and her husband flanking them on the steps of a church.

Another of Sarah and her husband, presumably taken a couple of years later because the baby had become a toddler, his wild tangle of curls framing a cherubic little face. They looked radiantly happy.

David smiled, fingering the photo, and then stilled.

Another photo caught his eye, this time of Emily, but again Sarah's husband was in the picture, and so was the little boy.

It was another wedding photo—a much simpler affair, the man looking drawn and weary, Emily smiling bravely, the little boy looking lost and rather sad.

The truth registered slowly. Anger flooded him as he stared down at the image, hot, blinding anger—and under it, connected somehow to his jealousy and pride, was relief. The child wasn't hers. Whatever had happened, it hadn't happened while their marriage bed was still warm.

Even so, she had deceived him now, lied, if only by omission.

He heard a footfall behind him and turned, photo in hand.

'When were you going to tell me?' he asked coldly. 'Or weren't you?'

* * *

Emily closed her eyes and sighed. She should have told him right at the beginning, but if she had she would have had no defence against him, nothing to protect her from the full force of his magnetism.

'I was going to tell you, of course I was. I had no reason not to,' she lied, and instantly remembered his remark about some women not being able to lie. Guilt must have written itself on her face ten feet high, because he snorted softly and put the photo down.

'So why not straight away?'

'Because it was irrelevant——'

'Irrelevant? You let me think you had conceived a child before our divorce was even final, and you think that's irrelevant?'

Jealousy, fierce and bitter, flooded Emily and drowned out all reason.

'You can talk,' she bit back. 'Within six months you were living with that damn blonde!'

He jerked as if she'd struck him, angry colour flooding his face. 'So what?' he said softly. 'At least I didn't do it for money.'

Emily's eyes widened in shock, and before she could turn away she felt the first tears well up and spill over.

'Bastard—get out!' she whispered.

'With pleasure,' he said coldly, and, brushing past her, he let himself out of the door.

'Emily, would you and Dr Trevellyan like——? Oh, he's gone! Emily?'

She stood frozen, her arms wrapped round her waist, hugging herself.

'Emily?' Mrs Bradley repeated softly, and, coming round in front of her, she tutted and folded her against her ample bosom. 'Oh, dear. I wondered if it was such a good idea you going out, but when he came with the plant and the bottle of wine——'

Emily sniffed and lifted her head. 'When?'

'Tonight—housewarming present, he said. It's in the kitchen.'

She went out to the kitchen and saw a lovely miniature rose smothered in blossom. Was it just coincidence that it was a deep, glorious red?

The blooms blurred, and she blinked hard to clear her vision.

'We always fight,' she said brokenly. 'Why do we always fight?'

She gave up with the blinking and turned her head into Mrs Bradley's comfortingly available shoulder.

'There, there, my treasure. You get it out of your system,' she crooned, and Emily allowed herself to indulge in a few seconds of luxury before straightening up and sniffing.

'Sorry,' she mumbled, and, fishing for a tissue in her pocket, she scrubbed at her cheeks and blew her nose.

'I ought to talk to him,' she said.

'He's still outside,' Mrs Bradley told her quietly.

'He is?' She peered through the window and saw his car still sitting by the kerb. She could just make out his figure at the wheel, but it was too dark to read his expression.

Was he still angry?

He probably had a right to be, she acknowledged. And anyway, it was hardly the first time he'd been angry with her. She could deal with it. Straightening her shoulders, she went to the door and opened it, to find David on the step.

'I was coming to apologise,' he said gruffly. 'That was a cheap shot. I'm sorry.'

She managed a wobbly smile. 'I was coming to apologise to you. It was none of my business who you were living with.'

'That's debatable,' he said, and his mouth quirked into a tentative grin that tugged at her heart. 'Can we call a truce?'

'We ought to talk. There's a lot to tell you, and I owe you that at least.'

'Do you mind if we talk inside?' he asked softly, and she blinked and stepped back.

'Of course—I'm sorry. Come in.'

She closed the door behind him and led him through to the sitting-room.

Mrs Bradley popped her head round the door. 'I've put the kettle on, or there's the wine in the fridge for you, and there's some cheese and biscuits on the side. I'm off to bed now.'

'Thank you, Mrs Bradley. Goodnight.'

'Goodnight, dear; goodnight, Dr Trevellyan.'

'Goodnight.'

They listened in silence to the soft tread on the stairs, and the slight creaking of the boards overhead. Then David sat at one end of the settee and turned to her.

'Sit down,' he told her.

She sat, twisting her wedding-ring on her finger, unable to look at him. She needed to explain everything to him, but it was where to start that was so difficult.

'Why don't you start at the beginning?' he said quietly.

So she did.

'Sarah and Philip were married the year we split up. He was very wealthy, ten years older than her, and his first wife had left him and taken him to the cleaners. He'd rebuilt his empire, straightened out his life and then when he met Sarah he fell for her like a ton of bricks.

'It was mutual, and within weeks they were married. A year later Jamie was born, and they asked me to be his godmother. I agreed.'

'Never imagining what it would lead to.'

'Oh, no, I never even dreamed I would end up fulfilling my obligation to James in that way. Don't get me wrong, I'm only too happy to do it, but at the time there was nothing to indicate that things would go so disastrously wrong.'

'It's a good job we don't know what's going to happen. Life would be intolerable if we were constantly counting down to tragedy.'

'Sometimes I think it's a relief,' she said quietly. 'If things are intolerable anyway, it must be a blessing to know it can't go on forever.'

David watched her silently, his eyes searching. 'Are you talking about Philip?'

She nodded. 'After Sarah died his life was hell. His life revolved around her and Jamie, and all he could think about was that he would die and Jamie would be alone.'

'Hence his proposal.'

'Yes.' She sighed softly. 'I was happy to accept it. At least that way I could make some reparation to Jamie for the loss of his mother.'

David regarded her oddly. 'Reparation?' he murmured. 'That's a strange word to use.'

She laughed, a hollow, empty sound in the quiet room. 'Not really. Sarah died because of me.'

'What?' David shifted round so that he was facing her, his eyes trained on her face, missing nothing. Emily looked away.

'She came to see me. She had just found out that Philip had cancer of the stomach and that it was inoperable. She was devastated. Jamie was four, she was thirty, and her whole life lay in ruins at her feet.'

'It must have been dreadful for her.'

Emily sighed. 'It was. Unbelievably awful. I've never seen such desolation in anyone's eyes—until I saw Philip after she'd died.'

David's hand curled round hers and squeezed comfortingly. 'So what happened?'

'It was foggy—great banks of impenetrable fog rolling up the valleys. I begged her not to go, to ring Philip and stay the night with me, but she refused. She said even one night away from him now was one night too many when every one of them was numbered.'

'So you let her go.'

'I should have made her stay,' Emily whispered. 'I should have phoned Philip myself and made him talk to her, but the fog wasn't so bad near me and I knew she'd be careful.'

'And?' he prompted after a moment.

'It was the other driver's fault—he'd been drinking,' she told him in a quiet monotone. 'The post-mortem revealed his blood alcohol was way over the limit. He crossed the central reservation and smashed into her car. She didn't stand a chance.'

His hand tightened on hers, and with a muffled sound she turned her face into his shoulder, burrowing her fingers into his jumper and hanging on, as if she could ride out the pain better in his arms.

He held her gently, rocking her against his chest, his hand smoothing her hair while he murmured softly against her ear.

Eventually she relaxed against him and he eased her closer so that her side was firmly against his and his arm lay loosely round her shoulders.

'Poor Em,' he murmured. 'You do know it wasn't your fault, don't you? She was an adult, fully capable of making her own decisions.'

'But she wasn't!' Emily lifted her head and met his eyes. 'She was so upset she was hardly in any state to drive. She wasn't crying—it was deeper than that. I think she was still in shock. As a doctor I should have recognised that.'

'Don't flagellate yourself with if onlys. It wasn't your fault she died. It was the other driver. It could have happened just as easily on a clear night, or in broad daylight.'

'That's what Philip said, but I still feel guilty. If I'd made her stay, she'd still be alive today.'

'That's what I meant about not knowing. I could be killed on the way home tonight, or shot in the surgery tomorrow by an aggrieved patient—anything could happen.'

'Don't!' she cried softly, and his eyes narrowed and searched her face.

'Don't tell me you still care, Em,' he said softly.

'Of course I care! I wouldn't want you to die, however bad our marriage was.'

'Was it so bad?'

His voice was hushed, wistful, almost yearning. How

she wished they could turn back the clock and try again.

'No,' she said softly. 'No, it wasn't so bad—at least, not for a long while. It only really fell apart at the end.'

His knuckles traced the line of her jaw, sending fire racing along her veins.

'I still loved you, even then,' he confessed.

'So why send me away?' she asked, her voice raw.

'God knows,' he said heavily. 'We were both on overload—working a hundred and twenty hours a week, hardly ever at home at the same time, too exhausted to speak to each other—we didn't stand a chance.'

There was a pause—a heavy, breathless pause, then he spoke again.

'We would now, though. We're older, wiser—we could try again.'

She eased out of his arms. Even though what he was suggesting was straight out of her own thoughts, still she knew it was impossible.

'It wouldn't work,' she told him. 'I have Jamie to think about. He must come first. I couldn't expose him to the possibility of any more heartache.'

'Why do you assume that if we got back together it would mean heartache for him?'

She stared at him in surprise. 'Well, of course it would. When you decide it's all too much effort and chuck us out——'

His eyes flickered shut, but not before she saw the pain in them.

'I'd never do that again. Anyway, I'm not suggesting we move in together yet or anything like that—just that we give ourselves time to find out if we still have something there worth working on.'

'Did we ever?' she asked bleakly.

'Oh, Emily—did it mean so little?'

Tears filled her eyes. 'Not to me. It wasn't me that moved in with someone else almost immediately.'

'Josie,' he said flatly.

'Was that her name?'

He nodded. 'Yes—that was her name. She was an SHO too—attached to the other surgical firm. She was attracted to me, and told me so. I was lonely—I took her out several times, and then she got fed up with pussyfooting around and took me back to the flat and tried to seduce me.'

'Tried?'

He laughed, a forced, painful little sound. 'Tried. She failed—or rather I did. I ended up lying in her arms crying my eyes out. Very romantic.'

'Oh, David. . .'

'She mopped me up and made me coffee and let me pour my heart out for hours, and then she told me she didn't think I ought to be living alone—I think she imagined I might do something stupid. Anyway, the upshot of it was that she moved into the spare bedroom and mothered me for the next two years.'

Emily was amazed. It was too fantastic not to be true, but why would any woman want to do that?

'Why?' she asked now.

'Why? Search me. All I know is I probably wouldn't have survived without her. I don't say I'd have tried to top myself, but I might well have starved to death or succumbed to food poisoning.'

They shared a smile of remembrance. David's housekeeping skills were strictly limited to boiling the kettle. In fact, Emily thought, looking at him, she wondered how he looked so well now unless he ate out all the time.

'I've improved,' he told her, as if he'd read her mind. 'I can't cook anything fancy, but the odd bit of steak or a grilled trout isn't beyond me any more, and even I can manage a salad and oven chips.'

Their eyes met, the rueful humour in them fading to a gentle regret.

'What happened to us, Em?' he asked gruffly. 'We were so happy at first. Was it just pressure?'

His hand came up and smoothed her cheek, and she turned her face into his palm, pressing her lips to the warm, dry skin. 'I don't know,' she mumbled. 'Maybe our love was never destined to last.'

'So why do I still love you now?' he asked softly.

Her eyes widened and she straightened up, searching his face.

'You don't,' she assured him.

'Oh, but I do.'

'No,' she protested gently. 'You might think you do, but it's just nostalgia. Once we see more of each other we'll be fighting again in no time flat. You'll see. We're incompatible, David. You know that.'

'Do I?'

'Don't you?'

'No. I love you. I've missed you. The last eight years have been a living hell.'

The gruff sincerity of his voice made her eyes fill. 'Oh, David,' she whispered. 'Don't say that. I've missed you so much.'

'Oh, Em——' He pulled her back into his arms, rocking her firmly against the hard expanse of his chest.

'You've ruined me for anyone else, you realise that, don't you?'

She twisted round and met his eyes, unable to believe what he was saying. 'What?'

'There's been no one else. After the fiasco with Josie my ego was too battered to try again for years, and then when I felt confident enough to try again I found I didn't want any other woman. None of them matched up to you.'

'But—it's been eight years. . .'

'I know.'

She was stunned. That David, of all people, could have abstained for eight years was beyond her comprehension. He had always been eager for their love-making when they were married—but then, so had she, and there had been no one for her since, either; even with Philip, whom she had married, there had been no intimacy, certainly not at first, and later, when their affection had grown, he had been too ill.

No wonder, then, that the kiss in the car had inflamed them both so rapidly and to such an extent.

'I want to kiss you again,' he said softly now.

'No,' she moaned, but he tilted her head gently and brought his lips down against hers, brushing them lightly until she yielded to his demands and opened her mouth.

With a ragged sigh he settled his mouth more firmly against hers and gave in to his instincts. His tongue sought hers and found it, suckling it, teasing it, playing tag until he grew bored and eased away, drawing her bottom lip into his mouth and suckling on it, biting it gently and then soothing it with his tongue.

By the time he lifted his head she was almost sobbing with need.

'I have to go,' he said almost roughly.

'No,' she pleaded.

'Emily, for God's sake,' he groaned, and then his hands were in her hair, his mouth clamped on hers again, their tongues embroiled in a mad dance that led to damnation.

Her body ached for him, her hands sliding feverishly under his jumper to seek the warm, firm planes of his chest.

As her fingers threaded through the soft hair he shuddered, his body trembling under her hands, and his own hands cupped her bottom and pulled her hard against him.

'Feel what you do to me,' he muttered harshly. 'Damn it, Emily, let me go before we do something we'll both regret.'

She pulled her hands away reluctantly, and as he sat up she let her eyes drift shut. Anything rather than look at him, see the flush lying on his cheekbones, the wild light in his eyes, the soft fullness of his mouth reddened from their kisses——

'Stay there. I'll see myself out.'

She listened as the door closed softly behind him, then toppled over on to the settee, still warm from his body. Hugging a cushion against her chest, she let the tears of frustration and anguish fall unheeded.

He wanted to try again. Dear God, so did she, but could she risk her heart? If it had hurt the first time, how much more could it hurt her now?

She buried her face in the cushion to muffle the sobs. Her body throbbed and ached, her heart felt as if it would burst—and upstairs, sleeping peacefully, was the reason she dared not try again.

CHAPTER FOUR

THE following morning Laurence Allen took her up to the cottage hospital to show her round. The practice took it in turns with another group in the little town to man the small casualty clinic, and each practice was responsible for its own patients in the hospital. Every day one member of the practice would visit the wards and check on the in-patients in their care, and the casualty rota was worked out on an alternating basis.

It was a pleasant little hospital, Emily thought, overlooking the wide stretch of the Bristol Channel. There was a glassed-in balcony attached to each of the wards where patients could have their meals if they were able to get up and about, and where they could sit during the day and look out over the changing sea.

On a clear day, Laurence told her, it was possible to see Wales. Today, however, there was a slight mist rolling across the water—a mist the colour of David's eyes, she thought absently, and had to drag her thoughts back in line for the umpteenth time that day.

There were eighteen beds in each of the four wards, two male and two female, and most of the beds were taken up by the elderly.

'It's halfway between a cottage hospital and a convalescent home,' Laurence told her. 'We use it for respite care, for those needing a bit more medical attention than it's possible to give them at home and for those who've been in Barnstaple at the North

Devon General and are making progress but still need hospitalisation.'

'It's a long way to travel to visit them in Barnstaple,' Emily said thoughtfully.

'It is, and people whose relatives are finding the travelling a bit much are very grateful to have this facility. We also have the odd maternity case. I don't know how long we can keep it going, though, but now we hold our own funds we can juggle where we spend the money and it stands more chance now, I suppose, provided we all agree it should remain.'

'And don't you?'

'Mostly,' he said, but didn't elaborate. She had already heard David and Robin Black talking warmly about the hospital, so assumed it must be someone from the other practice who was against the facility. Strange, she thought, because without it the demands on the medical and community staff would be much more intensive, let alone the inconvenience to relatives and the burden on the North Devon General.

'We're in the process of setting up a new scheme of emergency cover, based at the hospital, where one doctor runs an emergency clinic from after surgery till midnight every night at the hospital.'

'What about access to notes?' Emily asked, seeing pitfalls.

'No problem,' Laurence told her. 'Because the notes are all computerised, we can access them through a modem and there isn't the problem of having to cart notes around and then update the computer in the morning after home visits, and most of the patients seem quite happy with the scheme. It's cut down the number of house calls at night dramatically during our trial run, but we still run the normal service at the weekend except for a surgery Saturday and Sunday mornings. Still,' he said with a laugh, 'we're getting our patients trained. They don't call us out if they can come to us, and they get better treatment in the hospital because we've got the facilities there on the spot.'

'Makes sense.'

Laurence beamed at her. 'So glad you agree. Actually it was Maureen who thought of it—she's a real stalwart. You'll meet her in a minute. Let's go and do the clinic—want to give me a hand?'

'Sure,' she agreed.

They made their way down to the small casualty area, where the few patients had already been screened by a nurse and some had been treated without the need for medical assistance.

There was one query fractured toe, a dislocated shoulder and a splinter in an eye that needed their attention.

While the lady with the injured toe was being X-rayed, Laurence talked to the man with the dislocated shoulder.

'So, how did you do it?' he asked.

'Damn bull—I should've known better'n to try and hold the gate when he charged it. Stupid great brute. Just caught me at a funny angle.'

'Mmm.' Laurence prodded gently and the man winced.

'Sore?'

He nodded.

'Has it happened before?'

'Oh, ar—often. Like I said, should've known better.

Just give it a wrench, Doc. That's all it needs. Slips back a treat.'

Emily was sceptical, but Laurence shrugged. 'On your own head be it. Are you sure you don't want an anaesthetic?'

The man laughed. 'What? Jostle me all the way to Barnstaple just for that? Give over.'

'We could give you a muscle relaxant.'

'No—don't worry, Doc. Just a quick jerk is all it takes. The wife's done it before now.'

'OK. Are you ready?'

He nodded.

'Dr Thompson, could you grip him round the chest and steady him for me?'

Laurence took the man's arm in a firm grip, placed his foot against the man's armpit and on the count of three he applied a steady, even pull and twisted, and the head of the humerous slipped neatly back into place.

The man swore softly under his breath, sweat beading his brow, and then a nurse appeared in the doorway of the cubicle.

'Oh, Harry, not you again!'

'Hello, Maureen! Come back to see you, my love, didn't I?'

'Oh, Harry. How did you do it this time?'

'Rufus charged the gate.'

Maureen sighed. 'Playing King Canute again, were you? That bull of yours needs seeing to if you ask me— and so do you.'

Harry chuckled. 'Going to strap me up again?'

Laurence Allen nodded. 'Put it in a sling, could you,

Maureen? Thanks. Oh, by the way, this is Dr
Thompson. Emily, Sister Maureen Whitaker.'

'Pleased to meet you—I gather you're a font of great
knowledge and even better ideas.'

Maureen chuckled. 'Did he say that? What's the
matter, Dr Allen? Trying to get me to work at the
practice again?'

'Maureen, would I?' Laurence's eyes twinkled.
'Anyway, you're much too valuable here.'

'And I wouldn't dream of giving up real nursing to
do smears and pre-school boosters. OK, Harry, let's
have you in the treatment-room. Oh, by the way, I've
put fluorescein in the eye, and the toe is fractured. The
plates are on the lightbox.'

'OK. I think I'll take a look at the eye first—unless
you'd like to do that?'

'I'll do whatever you want me to,' Emily told him.

'OK. Do the eye, could you? I forgot to bring my
glasses, and you need clear vision and steady hands for
eyes.'

Emily introduced herself to the man with the dam-
aged eye, who was sitting with it covered by a large
white handkerchief. He was in late middle age, and
said his name was Frank Dooley.

She led him into a treatment-room, and a staff nurse
came with her and produced a trolley already laid up
for eye examination.

She laid the man down and he removed the handkerchief, revealing a streaming, firmly shut eye.

The foreign body had induced a condition known as
blepharospasm, a big word, Emily always thought, for
an eye that insisted on staying very sensibly and firmly
shut while watering like mad to wash out the foreign

body—and who could blame it? However, her first task was to persuade the man to allow her to open the eye, a mildly unpleasant procedure, so that she could examine it and anaesthetise it before removing the splinter, if indeed there was one.

Once she coaxed him into co-operation, she could see the splinter quite clearly, but under ultraviolet light the stain of the fluorescein showed no further corneal damage, thankfully.

'How did you manage it?' she asked conversationally as she carefully scanned the cornea.

'Chopping logs—my wife thought it might be nice to have a fire.'

'So when did you do it?'

'Last night. Thought it would pass, but it's been like this all night, so I thought it was time to come.'

'Past time,' Emily told him, but there was no damage done by waiting, luckily, as there might have been if the foreign body had been contaminated.

She flooded his eye with anaesthetic, waited a few moments until she could see that the eye was relaxing, then, using a sharp spatula called an eye spud, she carefully scraped the splinter out and then lifted it clear of the eye.

'Got it,' she announced, and the man sighed with relief and closed his eye.

'We'll cover it and keep it under wraps for a few days, and you'd better have some antibiotic drops with hydrocortisone in—it's called Neo-Cortef, and it'll reduce the inflammation and combat any possible infection. Whose patient are you?'

'Dr Allen's practice.'

'Oh. Right, well come in—where are we now?

Tuesday. Come in on Friday and let one of us have a look, and we'll go from there. OK?'

'Thank you, Doctor.'

She left the nurse dressing the eye and went out to find Laurence.

He was lounging in the office with Maureen, chatting over a cup of coffee.

'Perfect timing,' Maureen said to her, and pushed a full cup towards her.

'Oh, thanks. Life-saver.'

'How's the eye?'

'OK. I got the splinter out, no further damage, he's coming in on Friday for a check.'

'Good girl,' Laurence said approvingly. 'Right, finish your coffee and we'll get round the wards and see the old dears while we're here. Oh, has Amy Richardson had her baby yet?'

'No. I think she's hanging on for Christmas,' Maureen said with a twinkle.

'But it's September!' Emily said with astonishment.

'Only joking. She goes over every time. She's only got two more days before she has to go to Barnstaple to be induced, so I'm fully expecting her to walk twenty miles or something to get it going.' Maureen laughed. 'She'll try everything. One time it was Chinese take-aways, another lots of nookie—mind, that one worked.'

Laurence chuckled. 'And it's more fun than a twenty-mile walk.'

Smiling, Emily followed him along the corridor to the wards, where she was introduced to many of the patients.

'Don't try and remember them all,' Laurence advised.

Good job, Emily thought later when she was back at the surgery, because she could remember hardly any of them at all.

She did find she had one patient that day she remembered, however—Neil Blake. She couldn't imagine what he wanted, but he didn't make her wait.

'How long is this condition of my wife's going to last?' he asked her directly.

Condition? Emily thought. What condition?

'What has she told you?' Emily asked, playing for time.

'Just that until it's cleared up it's better to avoid sex, but once it's sorted we should be able to have a baby without any problem. Trouble is, when I asked her how long it would take, she got very vague. I wondered if you could help.'

Emily let out a mental sigh. Clearly the woman had told her husband a tissue of lies to hide behind, which would have been fine if he weren't here now asking her to explain. And Mrs Blake must have known he would come in—hence her question about confidentiality and him never knowing what had taken place.

Well, whatever the woman's motives, Emily was bound by the rules of confidentiality, so her secret was safe.

'I'm sorry,' she said to the man. 'I'm afraid I can't discuss your wife's condition with you without her consent——'

'She hasn't got anything wrong with her, has she? She's lying to me.'

'Mr Blake, I'm sorry, I really can't discuss it with you——'

'Damn the woman! I knew it!' He stood up and paced across the room, then whirled to face Emily. 'It's true, isn't it? She's having an affair.'

Emily sighed. 'Mr Blake, what goes on between you and your wife is nothing to do with me. I would say, though, that you didn't seem to be communicating very well yesterday when you came to see me.'

He snorted rudely. 'Dr Thompson, we don't communicate.'

'Then don't you think it would be wise to learn how to before you consider the idea of another child?'

He was silent for a moment, then he met her eyes with a level look. 'There isn't anything wrong with her, is there? Don't bother to answer; I know you can't say anything. And don't worry, I won't tell her I've been here. I won't trouble you any more. Thank you, Dr Thompson, you've been very patient.'

He left, and Emily sighed and pushed back her chair. He had been the last patient in a long and trying day, made more so by the almost total lack of sleep the night before.

The few hours of sleep that hadn't eluded her had been filled, like her waking hours, with David—only while she slept there was no rein on her emotions or her imagination.

How she was going to cope with working alongside him every day was difficult enough to fathom. If he decided to launch a sensory offensive, bombarding her with romantic gestures and tender little moments, coping would be wellnigh impossible.

And if he persisted in telling her that he loved her. . .

A tap on the door jerked her back to reality.

'Come in,' she called, and her heart thumped when she realised it was David.

'Hi.'

'Hi,' she managed.

'How are you?'

She looked away from him. His eyes were too searching, too all-seeing for her comfort.

'OK.'

He made himself at home on the edge of her desk, his lean thigh inches from her hand. She shifted it slightly before it disobeyed her and reached across to stroke the fine wool of his trousers stretched over taut, hard muscle.

'What did Neil Blake want?'

She blinked, trying desperately to concentrate. 'Neil Blake?'

'Yes—he just came to see you.'

'Um—he wanted to know how long his wife's condition was going to last.'

'Oh, hell.'

'Precisely. I told him I wasn't at liberty to divulge that information, and he had a fit. Said it was true, she was having an affair, and then told me he didn't expect me to say anything and he wouldn't tell her he'd been to see me.' She looked up at David. 'Actually, he sounded very sad.'

David nodded. 'I think he probably is. He's a faithful sort of type—not the last of the great romantics, but a good husband for all that. He doesn't really deserve this—as far as one can tell. It's difficult to judge from outside a relationship, of course—God knows it's difficult enough to judge from inside!'

She glanced down at her hands, twisting her wedding-ring again. 'Yes,' she murmured. 'It is—very difficult.'

His hand picked hers from her lap, his finger rubbing gently over the ring. 'Is this Philip's?'

She shook her head. 'No. No, it's yours.'

'Emily?' His fingers tipped her chin, bringing her eyes up to meet his. 'Indulging in sentiment?'

'I never took it off. Philip gave me another ring. I wore them together.'

Something strange happened in his eyes, something that could have been to do with pride and yet was strangely humble.

'Come for a walk with me this weekend—you and Jamie. We'll take the dogs down to Hunter's Inn and give them a run beside the river.'

'No.'

'Why? He ought to see the area. Can you remember the way?'

'I'll find it—I can map-read.'

He grinned, a little off-centre. 'So you can. I just thought it might be nice for him to have the company of the dogs.'

Wonderful for her, too, to have David's company—and with Jamie there she would be safe from the sensuous assault. She felt her defences crumbling.

'Don't try and work your way into his affections,' she warned.

'Is that a yes?'

His grin broadened, and something bright and beautiful lit his eyes. 'Thank you,' he whispered, and, bending foward he captured her lips in a fleeting kiss.

Seconds later, the door closed softly behind him.

* * *

She was on duty the following night, the Wednesday, and went up to the hospital for the emergency clinic. It was fairly quiet, but there was a steady stream of patients and she realised it would have been quite a hectic night had they all been house calls.

The odd one or two, of course, had used her as a convenient after-hours surgery, but it didn't really matter. She was there anyway, and if it meant they didn't have to take precious hours off work it couldn't really be a bad thing.

She was just packing up at midnight ready to go home when a car pulled up outside and a heavily pregnant woman was helped out and led into the reception area.

'Don't tell me—you're Amy Richardson.'

'Oh—you've heard about me.'

Emily smiled. 'Twenty-mile walk today?'

'No—five. I did fifteen yesterday.'

She paused, leaning against her husband and breathing lightly and quickly for a minute.

'It's obviously worked,' Emily said with a grin. 'Shall we take you through to the maternity-room?'

'I think that might be a good idea,' her husband said. 'She always hangs on, but once she starts there's usually no holding her.'

'How many have you got?' she asked as she led them through the quiet hospital.

'Four—this is five.'

'And definitely the last,' her husband added firmly.

'Spoilsport.'

'Amy, we're broke!'

Emily allowed herself a secret smile. There was broke, she mused, and broke. The BMW they had pulled up in was no more than a year old, the clothes they were wearing were far from chainstore seconds, and she'd lay odds that the children would have a private education.

The staff nurse on duty called the community midwife while Emily called up the notes on the computer and decided there was no need for her to panic.

Not that she was about to. The woman was clearly as strong as an ox, very used to childbirth and extremely sensible. And anyway, obstetrics was Emily's favourite speciality.

The midwife arrived just as Amy was settled into bed, and she examined her and told Emily that she expected no complications.

'You can go, if you like.'

Emily smiled. 'Do you want me to? I'm on call anyway, so I might have to leave, but I'd be happy to stay if you don't mind. I love babies.'

'Please yourself. You're very welcome. She'll do it without either of us.'

They shared a smile, and the staff nurse brought them all a cup of tea while they settled down to wait.

Amy didn't keep them long. By twelve-thirty she was getting to the end of the first stage, and at a quarter to one, with very little fuss and bother, the baby arrived, a lovely healthy boy.

'Oh, look at him, Jeremy! He's wonderful.'

'Another mouth to feed,' he grumbled, but his eyes were misted and he hugged his wife hard. 'Well done, darling.'

They turned their attention to the new arrival, and after the placenta was delivered they watched as the baby was cleaned up and checked.

'Super—they don't come better than that,' Emily said with a misty smile, and handed him back to his proud parents. 'Have you got a name for him?'

'David—what do you think?'

She swallowed the lump. 'I think that's a very good name.'

They celebrated his arrival with another cup of tea, and then Emily went home.

Even though she knew she ought to make the most of her few hours, she found it difficult to sleep. Her arms felt empty, her breasts ached, and low down there was an almost physical yearning in her womb.

Slipping out of bed, she went into Jamie's room and smoothed his hair back from his little face. She loved him dearly, but her body cried out for more.

Swallowing the tears that made her throat ache, she made her way back to bed, lay down and curled on her side, arms wrapped round her waist.

She wanted a baby, and not just any baby.

David's.

Need ripped through her, and with it anguish.

It wasn't fair! It was hard enough to resist him without her body joining forces with him and turning on her. Her biological clock, a gentle tick in the background until now, had suddenly begun to clamour.

It was a relief when the phone rang.

Saturday dawned clear, bright and with only a light breeze. It was a beautiful mid-September day, and she dressed Jamie in a thick tracksuit with a polo neck underneath. It was when she found herself vacillating over her own clothes that she pulled herself up short.

Jeans and a lambswool sweater would do fine, she told herself, and pulled them on just as the doorbell rang.

She tugged the sweater straight, flicked a brush through her hair and ran down to the hall to open the door.

He looked wonderful—tall, wind-swept, rugged— her heart crashed against her ribs until she was sure he'd see it through the fine wool of her sweater. 'Come on in—we're almost ready.'

He followed her into the kitchen where Jamie was sitting at the table with Mrs Bradley, eating cornflakes.

'Jamie, this is Dr Trevellyan. David, my son James.'

The introduction was deliberate, and David acknowledged her choice of words with a wry smile before turning his attention to the boy.

'Hello, James.'

'Hello,' Jamie mumbled round a mouthful of cereal.

'Don't talk with your mouth full,' Mrs Bradley said instantly, and softened the reprimand with a smile. 'Eat up, love, you'll keep the dogs waiting.'

He shovelled the food in quicker, clearly enthusiastic. David greeted Mrs Bradley, refused a cup of coffee and watched Emily as she slid her feet into trainers.

'I think you'll need wellies—it can get a bit muddy down by Heddon's Mouth, although it's usually OK on the path. Jamie might want to cross the river, though, and in shoes you'd have a problem.'

'OK. We'd better take something else in case of accidents.'

David chuckled. 'Very wise. Small boys and water make a fairly lively combination.'

With a smile, she put the trainers into a bag and

tugged off Jamie's shoes, putting them in there too while he gulped down the last of his milk and dragged his hand over the back of his mouth.

'Can we go, Emmy?' he said, and the enthusiasm in his voice brought a lump to her throat. It was the first time he had been keen about anything since before Philip had died, and she had despaired of ever seeing him smile again.

Not that he was smiling now, but his face was certainly more animated than of late, and the way he was fidgeting from foot to foot was a clear indicator of his excitement.

She passed him his wellies and tugged her own on, straightening up to find David watching Jamie with a strange expression on his face.

She tilted her head enquiringly, but he shook his head and picked up the bag with their shoes in.

'Right, are we done? Don't expect them back for lunch, Mrs Bradley. I'll treat them.'

'All right, Dr Trevellyan. I'll see you later, then.'

They went out to his car, a Volvo estate, to find the two dogs sitting up in the back, their faces expectant.

'OK, chaps, let's go,' David said, and after strapping Jamie in the back he slid behind the wheel and they set off.

The drive took about twenty minutes, and they parked by the river at Hunter's Inn and took the track beside the old pub down towards the sea.

Jamie ran on with the dogs, completely fearless, and Emily watched him anxiously.

'He'll be fine, Emily. Don't worry.'

'He's been so withdrawn.'

'That's only to be expected. He's had a lot to cope with. He's a lot like Sarah.'

'Isn't he? He's got Philip's curly hair, but otherwise he's the image of his mother.' She sighed. 'Sometimes I don't know if coming here was the right thing. Perhaps we should have stayed in Surrey, but he seemed to want to come to the cottage. They came here on holiday quite often before Sarah was killed, and I think his memories of it are all happy.'

'I'm sure that's very important, for him to remember the good times. We all need to do that.'

Emily swallowed. Just recently she'd been remembering the good times all too often, and her sleep had suffered as a result. She decided to change the subject.

'How are your parents?'

'Oh, OK. They've sold the farm. They're living in Putsborough now, near Croyde. They've got a little bungalow near the beach and they do B and B in the summer.'

'I can't imagine them without the farm,' Emily said thoughtfully. 'Do they miss it?'

'Dad does. Mum's relieved, I think. Of course they couldn't keep all the dogs, hence these two. Do you remember Bridie, the setter?' David asked. 'She would have been a puppy.'

Emily looked at the lovely red setter and nodded. 'Yes—your mother's dog.'

'Uh-huh. And Ruffian is Scoundrel's son.'

She remembered Scoundrel, too, a lovely Irish wolfhound with a wiry grey coat. Ruffian had the same coat, but a different, much more solid build.

'His mum was a Labrador—you never knew her. They've still got her, and Scoundrel, but when they sold the farm they had to cut back drastically. Three of the cats were found local homes, but they've still got two and the two dogs. Oh, and the donkey. We ought to take Jamie over and let him ride it.'

'He'd like that,' Emily said pensively.

'They'd love to see you again.'

The air was suddenly thick with tension. She stopped and turned to him, desperation showing in her eyes.

'David, please. Don't pressure me. I have to put Jamie first—even you can see that. Just now there isn't time in my life for trying to salvage a relationship that doesn't include him.'

'Of course it would include him,' David argued, but she shook her head.

'No. No, it wouldn't. I can't trust either of us, David, and there's no way I'd let him be hurt by our making a stupid mistake. I don't mind the odd walk like this, and I agree it's good for him to have the dogs to play with, but I won't have him hurt. Just remember that.'

His jaw worked, as if he was on the point of saying something, but then he turned on his heel, whistled the dogs and strode off towards the beach, leaving her trailing behind.

She caught up with them at the beach, to find Jamie playing inside the old lime kiln.

'Is it safe?' she asked worriedly.

'Of course. Jamie, come out now; let's go and have a look at the rock pools. There might be some sea anemones that can suck your finger. Have you ever touched one before?'

Wide-eyed, Jamie shook his head.

'Come on, then.'

David held out his hand, and after a second's hesitation Jamie slipped his smaller hand into it trustingly. Emily followed them over the rocks to the tideline, and watched as they crouched down, their two heads bent together, peering into rock pools.

'Here's one—give me your finger. It doesn't hurt; it's just like being kissed. Feel.'

'Oh!'

A delighted giggle broke loose from the child, and he turned a radiant face up to Emily.

'Emmy, come and try! It's really funny!'

A lump forming in her throat, she approached the boy and the man she loved. Crouching beside them, she let Jamie guide her finger into the open mouth of a sea anemone.

'It tickles,' she said, and her voice must have sounded odd because David shot her a strange look and then straightened up, leaving Jamie to his exploration.

'He's a lovely boy. You've taken on a hell of a lot.'

She took a steadying breath. 'I know. Still, I love him.'

David nodded. 'I can see that. You'll be good for him. I admire you.'

She almost wept.

CHAPTER FIVE

DESPITE Jamie's obvious enjoyment, Emily was glad when their outing came to an end. Watching him with David was too bittersweet to bear, and his thirst for masculine company brought back sad memories of Philip and Sarah.

All in all it was a melancholy mood she found herself in the rest of the weekend, and although she did her best to keep cheerful for Jamie she was glad when Monday came round again and she could get back to the busy routine of work.

And they were busy. After her first whole week, she was the subject of much curiosity and the influx of patients she had been expecting materialised as if by magic.

'You must be the most popular person in Biddlecombe today,' Sue told her cheerfully at their mid-morning break, and Laurence laughed.

'She's welcome to my patients, too. Just transfer them all to her—she's all they want to talk about—that and their piles.'

Chuckling, he put down his coffee-cup and left to go on his rounds. After seeing the last few patients in the emergency overspill clinic, her task today, Emily went on her own visits.

One was to a family in the area on holiday, and the man was complaining of pain in his shoulder. As he was the only driver and his wife felt he was unable to drive, Emily went to see him.

The pain turned out to be in the upper right side of his chest, had started quite suddenly and was worse when he breathed in, he said.

'Where were you when it started?' she asked him.

'We were going out—the car wouldn't start, and I had to push it while my wife sat inside to bump-start it.'

Emily examined him thoroughly, checking his pulse for irregularities, listening to his chest and sounding it for any unusual resonance, and came to the conclusion that he had probably strained his pectoral muscles. However, because of the danger of myocardial infection, she decided he ought to go to the hospital and have an ECG. 'I'll get the ambulance to pick you up,' she told him, and, having prescribed paracetamol for the pain, she left.

On returning to the surgery she went and found Robin Black, who was just on his way out for lunch.

'What should I do about this man?' she asked him. 'He's a temporary resident, but I don't want him dying of cardiac problems because I've just assumed he's strained his chest.'

'No, quite right,' Robin agreed. 'What about pneumothorax?'

She shook her head. 'No, I don't think so. It could be, but there was no reduction in breath sounds or hyper-resonance.'

'There might not be if it was small,' Robin said thoughtfully. 'I reckon you're probably right, but he ought to come in for an ECG. Have you asked transport to pick him up?'

She nodded. 'Sue's organised it.'

'Good. He'll need the temporary residence form filled in—it's probably got a number but I'm damned if I can remember it.'

'All done.'

'Good girl.' He grinned. 'Maureen will do the ECG and you can go up and check it out later. She'll see to all the details if you ring her.'

'Sue's done that, too.'

'Marvellous woman. I don't know what we'd do without her.'

'Maureen or Sue?'

He laughed. 'Either, but I meant Sue. Right, I'm off. Jill's expecting me for lunch.'

Emily, who didn't have time for lunch, felt her stomach growl in protest at the thought. She ought to grab a sandwich, but there never seemed to be time.

She finished her visits and made her way up to the hospital where she found Mr Warren in the waiting area with his wife and children.

'How is it now?' she asked him.

'Oh, pretty grim. It's getting worse if anything.'

He looked as if he was in pain, and Emily went into the office with Maureen and studied the ECG.

'It looks quite normal,' she said, puzzled but relieved. 'So not his heart, then.'

'No. How about a pneumothorax?'

Emily shrugged. 'I checked him for symptoms, but he seemed OK. I think I'll have another look, see if anything's got more obvious. Perhaps he's dislocated a rib or got intercostal neuralgia from a thoracic subluxation.'

'Pulled a muscle, even.'

'That's what I thought at first, but it shouldn't deteriorate.'

'No. Do you want me to get a bed ready?'

Emily glanced through the door at the man, now hunched over, his arms round his chest.

'It might be a good idea. That pneumothorax is looking more and more likely. Have we got a radiographer in?'

'Yes—do you want some pictures?'

'Yes, please. I'll write up the forms if you could contact her.'

'Sure.'

A few minutes later the diagnosis was confirmed on X-ray. A small, dark patch over the top of his right lung clearly indicated that air had leaked into the pleural space and was compressing his lung, causing the pain and the breathlessness he was now experiencing. It wasn't a large enough leak to justify putting in a chest drain, but Emily thought she could aspirate it with a needle.

Once he was transferred to a treatment-room, she infiltrated the site of the puncture with local anaesthetic and, using a large syringe and needle, she was able to remove most of the air, relieving his symptoms. The rest would absorb given time.

'I'm afraid you should probably spend the night in here just to be on the safe side, and the rest of the week very quietly. Have you got holiday insurance?' she asked.

He shook his head. 'No. Didn't think we'd need it.'

Emily found his wife discussing bus services to and from the area of their holiday cottage, which fortunately was in the town and so not too difficult for her to cope with the children and visiting. They might even manage to have a bit of a holiday, especially if he made a good recovery, but she was concerned about him driving them all back to London at the end of the week.

'We'll have to see how he is by then,' she told the woman, and then, having filled in the necessary papers for his admission, she made her way back to the surgery.

Once there she told Robin the outcome, and congratulated him on his diagnosis. 'How is it that everybody but me was looking for it?' she asked wryly.

'Because you were looking for something much more sinister,' he said with a laugh. 'Oh, well, it's sinister enough to wreck their holiday.'

'It must happen a lot,' she mused.

'Oh, yes. All the time, especially in the height of the summer. Tourism is our main product round here— that and clotted cream, and that's mainly for the tourists!'

'Oh, that reminds me, there's some clotted cream in the fridge for you and Laurence, Emily,' Sue told her. 'Courtesy of Harry Orr and his dislocated shoulder.'

'Oh, how kind. Jamie will love it.'

Jamie did—and so did Emily and Mrs Bradley. They abandoned sensible eating that night and feasted on scones and rich yellow clotted cream, and if Emily felt a touch queasy that evening she thought with satisfaction that she had only herself to blame.

Roy Warren and his pneumothorax made excellent progress over the next few days, and by the end of the week she felt confident letting him drive them all home.

She felt less confident, however, about David and

her relationship with him, particularly when he asked her again if they could go to his parents on Saturday afternoon so that Jamie could ride the donkey.

'They'd love to see you again, Emily. They're lonely now—it would make them so happy to see you and to have young Jamie to spoil for a couple of hours.'

'I'm not sure,' she told him, and promised to think about it, but despite her misgivings they did end up going to see the Trevellyans in Putsborough, and Jamie spent ages patting the donkey and sitting on its back while David's father patiently walked him up and down.

Emily would have hovered anxiously but Mrs T collared her and removed her to the kitchen.

'Help me with the scones,' she instructed, and although Emily knew full well that the woman needed no help at all she allowed herself to be engineered.

Anyway, it would be lovely to spend time with her in the kitchen again. They had done it so many times in the past, and if it brought a lump to Emily's throat, well, so what? So did everything else she seemed to do these days.

'You're looking well,' Mrs T said, eyeing her with undisguised curiosity. 'I was sorry to hear about Sarah—and her husband. It was very brave of you to take the child on, knowing you'd be alone.'

'I'm not really,' she protested. 'Mrs Bradley's there all the time—actually, she could probably cope perfectly well without me.'

Mrs T made a non-committal noise and plopped the bag of flour on the worktop. 'He seems a nice child.'

'He is.'

'David would have made a good father, you know.'

Emily's eyes found him through the window, hands thrust deep into the pockets of his old waxed jacket, the dogs sitting at his side.

'Yes, I know,' she said quietly. The biological ache started again, low down, and she almost groaned aloud.

'You should have had children. Maybe then you wouldn't have given up so easily.'

'Mrs T, please,' Emily pleaded, close to tears, and the woman sighed and backed off.

'Sorry. I didn't realise it still hurt you, too.'

She chewed her lip. 'David said there'd been no one else.'

'Not as far as I know, and I'm sure he would have said. Not since Josie, anyway. He hasn't seemed to want to bother.' She spooned flour into a bowl, cut a big chunk of butter off the block and dropped it in, then plunged her plump hands into the mixture. 'Of course, you know he wants to marry you again.'

Emily's heart thumped.

'Has he said so?'

Mrs T's hands stopped and she turned slightly, regarding Emily thoughtfully over her shoulder. 'Does he need to?'

She sighed. 'Probably not. Mrs T, I can't. I have to care for Jamie now, and I can't let my personal life influence my decisions about what's best for him.'

She snorted. 'Isn't it best for Jamie that his mother should be happy?'

'Exactly. David didn't always make me happy, Mrs T—nor I him. There were often times when we were both miserable.'

'Lack of communication.'

'Quite. What makes you think we'd be any better now?'

She snorted again. 'Seems to me a great waste of being alive if you don't bother to learn from your mistakes.'

'Meaning?'

She gave up any pretence of making the scones. 'Meaning that you'd try harder this time, make more effort to communicate your thoughts and feelings. Last time you made too many assumptions.'

'Perhaps you are now,' Emily said quietly. 'Perhaps it isn't what I want.'

'Still lying to yourself? Oh, well, you'll come round. He's got a persuasive tongue.'

Emily thought of his kisses, and flushed. Mrs T, however, had turned back to her scones and missed the tell-tale colouring, to Emily's enormous relief.

She set the table while Mrs T cut out the scones and popped them in the oven, then ladled out great dollops of clotted cream and home-made strawberry jam.

'They'll be ready in a minute,' she said, putting the kettle on. 'Better get the menfolk in. They'll all need to wash their hands.'

A tap on the window brought a nod of acknowledgment from the men in the garden, and David lifted Jamie down while his father led the donkey back to her stable and fed her.

They came in, Jamie beaming, and after a great production of hand-washing they settled down to have tea together. It was a cheerful, friendly meal, and Jamie ate hugely, to Emily's relief. He had been picky of late, but today he tucked into the ham sandwiches and scones and cream.

'He's eaten well,' Mrs T said as they were leaving.

'All that fresh air,' Mr T said with a wink, and Emily smiled at him.

'Thank you for letting him ride Topsy. I'm sure he's had a lovely time.'

'I have—thank you ever so much,' Jamie said, his eager face tipped up to David's father. 'Can we do it again?'

Mr T bent over and knuckled the boy's hair gently. 'Of course you can, son. Any time you like.'

'We'll see, Jamie. We don't want to be a nuisance.'

'He's not a nuisance—he's a delight, and more than welcome—and so are you,' Mr T added.

Emily looked helplessly at David, but he smiled innocently and let her struggle.

'You're very kind,' she managed, her voice choked.

'Come on, Jamie, let's strap you in,' David said finally, and opened the car door.

'Seems to me if you want the child to be happy you're worrying about all the wrong things,' Mrs T said. 'Give him a chance, Emily. He's a good man. He's older now, and wiser. And he does love you.'

She saw tears glitter in the older woman's eyes, and turned away. 'Thank you for a lovely tea,' she said as she climbed into the car. 'We'll be in touch, I expect.'

She shut the door, staring stonily ahead, and David climbed in beside her and started the engine, pulling away with a wave.

'She been giving you a hard time?' he said softly.

'What do you think?'

His hand came out and found hers, clenched tightly on her lap. 'I'm sorry. I should have warned her to leave you alone.'

'She means well.' The feel of David's hand on hers was warm and comforting, and she was almost sorry when they reached a junction and he removed it so that he could drive.

She didn't ask him in when they got back, and he didn't press it, just dropping them off and driving away.

Jamie watched them go, then turned to the house with a sigh. 'I wish we could have a dog like Ruffian or Bridie.'

'Maybe we can, one day,' she said. She'd been thinking about it for some time, and his whole-hearted response to David's dogs had made her more sure that it was the right thing to do. They were just so devoted and uncritical, she thought, loving you regardless of your mistakes and failings. Perhaps she ought to have one!

During the course of the following week she met Jenny Wellcome, the wife of the man who was having an affair with Ann Blake.

Her MS had flared up again, leaving her even weaker, and the spasticity in her limbs had increased despite the Baclofen.

As Emily drove up to the farm, she found herself curious to meet the man Ann Blake would sacrifice her marriage for, and the woman he was too devoted to to leave.

She was met at the gate by a man who introduced himself as Richard Wellcome. He was of medium height, balding, older than she had expected—not in any way the sort of person she would have anticipated would appeal to Ann Blake. And yet his eyes were filled with a wealth of kindliness, tinged with despair. There was a dog beside him, leaning against his leg, clearly his shadow.

'How is your wife?' Emily asked him.

He sighed, his shoulders lifting in a helpless shrug. His hand automatically found the dog's head and rested there, as if for comfort. 'She seems to be going downhill fast. I don't know—I just get the feeling she won't be here much longer.'

'I'm sorry,' Emily said quietly, and he met her eyes, his own full of sorrow.

'So am I. Whatever you might have heard, I do love her.'

'I know.'

They exchanged a smile of understanding, and she followed him into the little farmhouse.

Jenny was in a makeshift bed by the fire, a hoist near by for lifting her in and out, and as they went in she turned her head and gave a slightly lop-sided smile.

'You must be Dr Thompson. I'm Jenny Wellcome.'

'Hello, Mrs Wellcome.'

She crossed the room and took the frail hand in her own much stronger grip. 'It's nice to meet you. What can I do for you this morning?'

'I wanted to talk to you about something. I would have preferred to see David, but he wasn't on duty and I didn't feel it should wait. Richard, you couldn't make us a cup of coffee and then leave us for a while, could you, love?'

'Of course.'

He went quietly out, and they could hear him pottering in the kitchen, muttering gently at the dog who was obviously underfoot.

'Shall I check you over while I'm here? David tells me your Baclofen wasn't working and he'd increased the dose. Does the stiffness seem any better?'

'Oh, that Baclofen's hopeless. I drop things all the time now.'

'That may not be the muscle relaxant, of course.'

'You mean it could be another area of attack?'

'It's possible.'

'I don't think so. It doesn't feel the same. My legs have gone now, this time. I can't feel them at all, and I don't even know when I've wet myself any more.'

Her voice was flat, accepting, and Emily found her courage rather humbling.

Richard came back in then, set down the coffee and hovered anxiously.

'Can you manage it?'

'I'll help her,' Emily said with a reassuring smile. 'Don't worry. I'll come and find you before I leave.'

He nodded, kissed his wife with every appearance of devotion and left them alone.

'Have you been here long enough to garner the gossip?' Jenny asked after a moment.

'Gossip?' Emily said, dreading what was coming next.

'About Richard and Ann Blake?'

'I don't listen to gossip.'

'You should. They've been having an affair for months. She's a nice woman. Pity about the little girl, though.'

Emily didn't know what to say, but it seemed Jenny was quite happy with her silence.

'I understand, you know,' she told Emily. 'He's a very passionate man, and I'm no good to him any more—not like that. He's worried, too, about the farm. Things aren't good. He doesn't realise that I know, but he ought to sell up and cut his losses. He won't talk to me about it, though, because it's my farm and he doesn't want to worry me or let me down.' She gave a small, wry laugh.

'He's always unhappy after he's been with her. Guilty, I suppose. I know about guilt. I have to live with it every day. I'm ruining his life. If it weren't for me he would have been able to concentrate on the farm, maybe turn it around. This hoist was expensive, too, but it means I can get myself in and out of bed. Well, I could. I can't now, and most of the time it just stands there mocking me.'

She gave a shaky sigh. 'You can't imagine what it's like to lose your independence.'

'Oh, I can,' Emily assured her. 'My husband was very ill with cancer for nearly a year before he died, and he became very dependent by the end. I think I was closer to him then than I've ever been to anyone. We talked all the time. It was very important to us both, and I think he helped me to understand a great deal.'

'Richard and I used to talk,' she said softly. 'We used to discuss everything, but since I've been ill he carries everything alone. That's why I don't mind about Ann—he needs someone to lean on, and if it can't be me it might as well be her.'

Emily found her philosophical attitude and selflessness very humbling. To lie there and know you had lost your husband to another woman, without any weapons to fight for him, must be savagely painful.

She helped her drink her coffee, and when she set

the cup down and blotted Jenny's lips the woman smiled.

'Thank you. That was lovely.' Her eyes flicked across to the bureau beside the television. 'Could you do something for me? In that bureau, at the back, behind all the papers is a document. I want you to see it, and attach it to my notes.'

Emily got up and opened the bureau, pulling forward the clutter of old letters, bills and other paraphernalia until she found a sealed envelope.

'Is this it?'

Jenny nodded. 'Yes, that's the one. Open it.'

She sat down again on the edge of the bed and carefully slit the envelope, pulling out the single sheet of paper.

'It's a living will,' Jenny said quietly. 'I don't want any further treatment. I don't mind alleviation of my symptoms, I'm not heroic enough to want to suffer, but I don't want any treatment that will extend my life. No antibiotics, no other fancy drugs—enough's enough. We've all reached the end of our rope. When I come to the point where I'm no longer mentally competent, I want that document to stand as an advance directive of my wishes—and I don't want Richard overruling it.'

She had clearly done her homework, Emily thought as she scanned the document. 'Have you discussed this with your husband?' she asked.

'No. He wouldn't agree.'

'Maybe you should talk it over.'

'No.' The woman was adamant. 'He feels bad enough. I don't want him finding out—I want him to think it was inevitable. Anyway, nothing's going to happen for ages. It's just insurance.'

Emily was concerned. 'Please talk it over with him. It's your life, and if it's intolerable, then I believe you have the right to make a decision about prolonging it artifically, but I don't think it's a decision you should make alone.'

Jenny shook her head. 'You don't understand. Richard gets depressed. He's been ill. He can't cope with this sort of thing; he finds it too distressing. I wouldn't want him to have to carry the burden of being part of the decision.'

Emily nodded. 'OK. I'll talk to Dr Trevellyan. I imagine he'll want to discuss it with you himself, but I'll take it now and attach it to your notes.'

She put it in her bag.

'Richard'll want to know what we were talking about,' Jenny told her. 'Could you lie to him? Tell him I wanted to ask you about my periods and thought it might embarrass him?'

'Would it?'

She smiled. 'Possibly. You can just be evasive, if you'd rather, let me do the lying.'

Emily stood up and snapped her bag shut. 'I wish you'd tell him the truth.'

'No. Don't worry, I'll deal with him. Thank you for coming.'

'My pleasure. I'll see you again.'

She let herself out, and the dog gave a sharp woof and trotted over to her, followed more slowly by Richard.

'Everything all right?' he asked.

She nodded. 'Jenny just wanted to chat about something.'

'There's nothing new? Nothing I should know about?'

She decided to answer the first part of the question only. 'No, nothing new. She's unhappy with the Baclofen. It's a difficult compromise.'

'The whole damn thing's a difficult compromise,' Richard said heavily, and then forced a smile. 'Well, thank you for coming, Dr Thompson. And thank you for being so good with Ann the other day.'

She gave him a smile as forced as his own had been, but didn't answer. What could she say? Unhappy with the whole situation, she began to believe David was right when he said she should have as little to do with it as possible.

Climbing back into her car, she set off down the hill towards the surgery, and on the way passed David's cottage. His car was outside, and on imuplse she pulled up and went to the door.

He opened it almost immediately. 'Emily! Come on in.' He held the door for her, his face registering surprise. 'What brings you here?'

'This.' She pulled the document out of her bag, watched him scan it and then shrugged when he raised an enquiring eyebrow.

'She wanted to see you, really, but she didn't want to wait. I checked her over—there was no sign of an infection that I could see, but I wondered if she was feeling off colour and thought she'd get that in quick before she went down with flu or something.'

'She shouldn't—she's had a jab already. I know it's early, but she can't cope with that sort of infection.

Perhaps she's worried she'll get brainstem involvement and lose her ability to communicate. Had lunch?'

'No—no, I haven't.'

'I was just about to heat up some soup. Want to join me?'

'I ought to let the surgery know where I am.'

'Phone's there. Cream of chicken OK?'

'Fine.'

She rang the surgery and then followed him into the kitchen. Bridie lifted her head and wagged her tail, Ruffian opened one eye, yawned and carried on sleeping. She sat down at the table and watched David struggle as he sliced bread and laid it in a wire frame, then clamped it under the lid of the Aga. Perversely, he was heating the soup in the microwave.

As if he saw the irony, he grinned. 'Old meets new. The toast tastes better this way,' he explained.

He dished up, joined her at the table and then dipped a piece of toast into the soup. 'So, what did you make of the situation?'

'Awful.' She told him about her conversation with Jenny, and how she knew about the affair, and David sighed.

'Oh, dear.'

'She seemed very accepting.'

'Difficult to see how she could be anything else.'

'Mmm. Anyway, I said I'd talk to you about it.'

'Thanks. I'll go and see her. Have you forgiven my mother yet, by the way?'

She blinked. 'Your mother?'

'For the third degree.'

'Oh, that.' She laughed. 'It was nothing. She just

loves you, and she loves happy endings. It would be nice and tidy, I suppose.'

He made a non-committal noise and wiped his bowl with the last scrap of toast.

'That was delicious,' she said, to change the subject. 'Don't tell me you made it.'

'No, Mum did. She does batches for me for the freezer. Want some more?'

She shook her head. 'I ought to be getting back.'

'Why? They can call you. Have a cup of coffee and a bit of Mum's fruit cake.'

She gave a low laugh. 'You know just how to push my buttons, don't you? I love her fruit cake.'

'I know. Do you blame me for using underhand tricks?'

Suddenly the tension crackled between them. Their eyes were locked, their breath halted.

'I'm going to kiss you,' he warned, and, pulling her gently to her feet, he drew her into his arms and locked his hands together behind her back, easing her against him.

Desire, hot and sweet, sprang to life inside her. Mesmerised, unable to turn away even though she knew she should, she watched as his mouth came slowly down. As it closed over hers, her lids fluttered shut and a tiny sigh escaped her.

She gave up all attempts at reason, ignoring her conscience, her common sense, everything—nothing mattered any more, only the feel of his mouth, the warm, velvet sweep of his tongue, the hard jut of his body locked against hers.

The phone ringing in the background was shattering.

They broke apart, their breath dragged in in painful

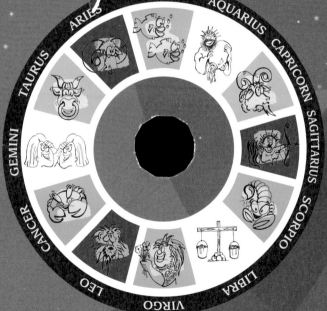

FREE! THIS CUDDLY TEDDY BEAR!

You'll love this little teddy bear. He's soft and cuddly with an adorable expression that's sure to make you smile.

PLAY THE MILLS & BOON
LUCKY STARS GAME!

Scratch away the silver panel. Then look for the matching star sign to see how many gifts you're entitled to!

 WORTH 4 FREE BOOKS, A FREE CUDDLY TEDDY AND FREE MYSTERY GIFT.

 WORTH 4 FREE BOOKS, AND A FREE CUDDLY TEDDY.

 WORTH 4 FREE BOOKS.

 WORTH 2 FREE BOOKS.

YES! Please send me all the free books and gifts to which I am entitled. Please also reserve a Reader Service subscription for me. If I decide to subscribe I shall receive four superb new titles every month for just £7.20 postage and packing free. If I decide not to subscribe I shall contact you within 10 days. The free books and gifts will be mine to keep in any case. I understand that I am under no obligation whatsoever. I may cancel or suspend my subscription at any time simply by contacting you. *I am over 18 years of age.*

12A4D

MS/MRS/MISS/MR _____

ADDRESS _____

_____

—————— POSTCODE _____

MORE GOOD NEWS FOR SUBSCRIBERS ONLY!

When you join the Mills & Boon Reader Service, you'll also get our free monthly Newsletter; featuring author news, horoscopes, competitions, special subscriber offers and much more!

◆ TEAR OFF AND POST THIS CARD TODAY! ◆

Mills & Boon Reader Service
FREEPOST
P.O. Box 236
Croydon
Surrey
CR9 9EL

NO
STAMP
NEEDED

gasps, eyes locked. Finally he turned and lifted the receiver.

'Trevellyan—yes, she's here.'

He held the receiver out to her, and pushed a pad and pencil towards her. Shaking, her hand refusing to co-operate, she jotted down the address of the patient and rough directions.

'I have to go,' she told him. 'A farming accident— Joe Hardwill?'

'Joe? I'll come. We'll take my car; it's a bit tricky to find.'

She went without question, and as they wiggled across Exmoor she was glad she didn't have to find the way herself. As they turned into the farmyard several dogs bounded to greet them, followed by a panic-stricken woman in her late fifties.

'Oh, Dr Trevellyan, thank God you're here. It's Joe—he's turned the tractor over in the top field. I think he's dead!'

CHAPTER SIX

JOE was still alive when they reached him, but he was in a serious condition and David was worried.

'When did it happen?' he asked the man's desperate wife.

'I don't know—I expected him in for his dinner at twelve. Well, he's never late, Doctor—not for his dinner. By twelve-thirty I was really getting worried, because his chest has been getting to him again.'

David frowned. The man's colour was poor, his lips slightly blue. He was lying under the huge mudguard of the tractor, but by a miracle he had been thrown into a hollow. Although he was trapped by the legs, his chest wasn't compressed unduly, and that gave him more chance. How long he'd been there, though, was anybody's guess. Something between one and three hours, Mrs Hardwill thought, since he had been in for breakfast at nine-thirty and had come out again at ten. It was now a little after one.

'The ambulance is on its way from Barnstaple,' Mrs Hardwill told them, 'and Sam next door is getting his tractor to lift the Fordson off, but—oh, Dr Trevellyan, tell me he's going to be all right.'

David straightened and squeezed her shoulder reassuringly. 'We'll do all we can. Why don't you go back and wait for the ambulance? They might be able to drive fairly close.'

With a brisk nod she turned away, her panic eased by the performance of a necessary task.

Keep everyone busy, give people a job to do to occupy their minds. It was the old training ethic of emergency procedure, and Emily was pleased to see it work on Joe's wife.

'What can I do?' she asked David.

'We need to get a line in and get some plasma expander into him. I think he's got multiple leg fractures, almost certainly—he'll need an op, and a good anaesthetic risk he ain't. We'd better do all we can for him, though.'

They worked in silence, except for the odd necessary comment, and by the time the intravenous line was in and fluid was running into him they could hear the ambulance approaching up the valley, its siren going.

'Good. Now all we need is to get him out and off to hospital. The orthopods can glue him together. Ah, here's the tractor.'

David stood up and waved to Sam, who manoeuvred his tractor so that it was on the other side, facing away, and then jumped down and ran round.

'How is he?'

'Rough. The ambulance is here. I think the best thing is to wait till they've got a stretcher, then lift the tractor a little and I'll crawl under and check him before we pull him out. I don't want you lifting it too far and doing any more harm if his leg is stuck in the wheel or anything.'

Emily's heart nearly stopped at his words. Crawl under? It could slip, lose traction in the mud and crash back down on him, killing him.

She bit her lip. There was no point in arguing. It was

her or him, and the men would all shoot themselves before they'd allow a woman to perform such a dangerous act. So she swallowed her fear, and when the time came she held the bag of plasma expander and her breath, and watched him as he wriggled face down in the mud to a point where he could see the legs.

'OK, lift a bit more—that's fine! Chock it at that point!'

They quickly pushed broad timbers under the tractor, wedging it up, and then David and the paramedic carefully eased Joe on to the stretcher and slid it out from under the tractor. He moaned slightly and then was silent again, and David's face was grave.

'Right, I think he needs to go in fast,' he said. 'Right tib and fib have gone, and the left femur, I should say. Maybe pelvis, too. He's a chronic bronchitic, recent bout of bronchitis that didn't respond terribly well to antibiotics. Probably pseudomonas. Oh, and he's a heavy smoker.'

'Aren't they all,' the paramedic grunted as he splinted the legs. 'Right, let's get him away before he comes round and starts to hurt.'

They loaded him into the ambulance, and Mrs Hardwill climbed in after them, a small, weary suitcase clutched in her hand.

'Poor old boy. Do you think he'll make it?' Emily asked as they followed the ambulance slowly back along the track to the farm.

'God knows. Probably not. He's a disagreeable old blighter, but he's got a certain amount of charm nevertheless.'

They reached the car, and David gave his clothes a cursory glance before getting into the car.

'You'll ruin the upholstery.'

'It's only mud. It'll brush off. The red earth round Wiveliscombe is much worse.'

She admired his philosophical attitude—and his courage. Suddenly, the danger passed, she began to shake almost uncontrollably.

'Are you OK?' he asked, turning his head to glance at her.

'Just reaction.'

'It was fairly gruesome. Sorry.'

'Not the accident,' she said, her voice unsteady. 'You crawling under that thing like that.'

He shot her another look, this one compounded of disbelief and curiosity. 'Worrying about me, Emily? Such progress.'

'Don't be stupid,' she muttered. 'I'd worry about anyone.'

His smile was wry. 'And there I was hoping it was because of your undying love for me.'

Little did he know. . .

Joe Hardwill survived the operation to pin his femur and plate his lower leg, but only just. He was in Intensive Care on a ventilator for over a week, and it was some time before the danger of pneumonia was past.

David went to see him in Barnstaple, and reported his disgust at having been unconscious and missing Emily.

'I think he's looking forward to meeting you,' David said with a teasing laugh. 'You'll have plenty of chance—once he's a bit better he'll be discharged to the cottage hospital under our tender ministrations.

You can go and make friends with him and try and persuade him to stop smoking.'

'He's not still smoking now!'

'He's trying—the sister caught one of his visitors giving him a crafty drag the day before yesterday. I think she nearly flayed him alive!'

'I should hope so! What an idiot!'

David sighed. 'Ah, Emily, he's just an old man. You'll like him. He says he hears you're the prettiest thing to happen to Biddlecombe since he brought his wife home forty years ago.'

She blushed and laughed. 'I hope you set him straight.'

'Oh, yes—I told him that, delightful though his wife was, you had her beaten into a cocked hat.'

'David! You didn't!'

He laughed. 'No, of course I didn't, but I could have done.' His face changed, the laughter giving way to something softer and infinitely more tender. 'Oh, Emily. I've missed you.'

'David, please. . . Not here.'

'Where, then?'

Her heart thumped. 'Nowhere. I've told you, it won't work.'

'Not if you won't give it a chance,' he agreed. 'Oh, well, you're right. This isn't the time or the place. I've got an antenatal clinic, and you've got a family planning clinic. We'd better get to it.'

The family planning clinic was interesting, a mixed bag of different ages and requirements.

She fitted an IUCD with the help of Eve Jenkins, the practice nurse, and then measured for, fitted and checked the insertion of a diaphragm, advised one woman of thirty-five who was an ex-smoker to come off the Pill and consider some other form of contraception, and then fitted another IUCD in a twenty-year old who was unable to take the Pill because of family history.

A busy afternoon, and by the time her surgery came round she was tired and hungry.

The last patient was a surprise. She was young, still fifteen, and came on her own without her mother. It was a general surgery, and Emily wondered what had brought her.

However, as soon as she came in, alarm bells rang. The girl looked so uncomfortable, almost as if coming had been a mistake. Emily tried to set her at her ease.

'Hello, Clare—can I call you Clare?' she asked.

She nodded, giving little away.

'So, Clare, what can I do for you?'

'Um—I wondered—can you put me on the Pill?'

Emily put down her pen, leant back in her chair and studied Clare's face. She looked embarrassed and awkward, as well she might, discussing this rather difficult topic for possibly the first time.

'How old are you?' Emily asked her, although she knew full well.

'Nearly sixteen.'

'And are you already in a sexual relationship, Clare?'

She nodded, blushing.

'And what are you doing at the moment about contraception?'

She shrugged diffidently. 'He uses something—well, mostly.'

'Mostly?'

'Well, sometimes he's run out.'

'You do realise that could get you pregnant?'

The girl's eyes were scornful as only a teenager's could be. She was also highly defensive.

'Of course—why do you think I'm here? Oh, it's hopeless—I knew you'd say no!'

She stood up and was about to flounce out of the room when Emily called her back.

'Clare, sit down and discuss this with me like a mature adult. That is, after all, how you want to be treated, isn't it?'

The girl subsided. 'Sorry.'

'That's OK. I know it's difficult. Now, there is one very important point I have to make. This boy that you're having the relationship with—you do both realise that he's breaking the law, don't you?'

She nodded. 'It's so outdated, though. Everybody does it these days.'

'I'm sure not everybody does,' Emily argued gently. 'It just seems like it. Now, there are all sorts of things I have to discuss with you. Do you know that being on the Pill can have side-effects?'

'Such as?'

She outlined the problems, the need to take it regularly and without fail, the physical and psychological effects of early intercourse, and the need to involve her parents in her decision.

'No!' she said to this last point. 'I couldn't! Dad'd kill him!'

'You must face the possibility that they could find out. What if they find your pills? Wouldn't it be better to have their knowledge and consent? They might not like it, but they are your parents and they love you. Doesn't their opinion matter to you?'

'They're old and stuffy—they wouldn't understand.'

Emily smiled gently. 'I think you might be surprised. If you tackle it head-on, like an adult, they might well respond better than if you sneak round behind their backs and they find out later by accident. Most parents do find out, you know.'

She was thoughtful for a moment, but then shook her head. 'No. They'd die, and so would Gran. I couldn't handle telling them. Put it like this—either you put me on the Pill or sooner or later I'll get pregnant by accident. It's a miracle it hasn't happened already.'

'Are you sure it hasn't?'

She nodded. 'Yes. I'm all right, I've just finished a period.'

'OK. I'll examine you, make sure everything's all right and ask you a few questions about your family history, then if I think you're able to take it I'll put you on a low-dose pill, but you must take it without fail, and if you forget or you have a tummy bug or feel sick or for any reason take it late you must use condoms for the rest of the cycle. On the other hand, you could, of course, have a diaphragm.'

'A cap? Yuck, no! One of my friends had one, and she said the cream goes everywhere and it stinks, and half the time she can't get it in—anyway, she's pregnant now, so that's no good!'

Emily gave up. The girl was clearly informed, knew what she wanted and was likely to get pregnant if she resisted prescribing. She examined her thoroughly, took a complete history and then prescribed a low-dose pill.

Repeating the warnings about taking it regularly,

and still with some misgivings, she sent the girl on her way.

Moments later David came in.

'Fancy a drink?'

'No, I must get back. Sorry. Perhaps another night.'

He looked disappointed, and for a second she regretted her refusal. Why shouldn't she go out for a drink with him? It hardly counted as a reconciliation, did it? And it couldn't harm Jamie.

'What did Clare want?'

'Oh—to go on the Pill.'

'What?'

She was startled by his reaction. 'Do you know her?'

'Yes—her grandmother lives with them and I visit her regularly. I know the whole family. Clare's often there. They'll go off the deep end, you know. I hope you've covered yourself in scrupulous depth.'

'Don't tell me—they're Catholics.'

'Catholics? He's a Baptist. He makes the average Catholic look like something out of Sodom and Gomorrah.'

Emily groaned. 'Oh, no. David, she's already sleeping with the boy.'

He sighed and stabbed his fingers through his hair. 'Well, God help you when her father finds out, is all I can say. What did you advise her?'

'Anything and everything but.'

'You could have simply refused.'

'And had another teenage pregnancy on my conscience? No way. I'll brave his wrath if necessary. He can only sue me.'

David laughed. 'Oh, Em. Come on, have a drink. You look as if you could do with it.'

She shook her head. 'What I could do with is a hot bath, a warm drink and a lazy hour by the fire.'

Something flickered in his eyes.

'Sounds inviting. Want to share?'

'David. . .'

Her protest was breathy and without conviction.

'We never did finish that kiss the other day,' he said softly.

She backed away, her heart thumping. 'Please—stop it. It's unfair.'

'I quite agree. I don't know why we keep beating about the bush. Perhaps we should just get it out of our systems. Then maybe we could both get on with our lives.'

He turned on his heel and strode away, frustration in every line of his body, and Emily sagged against her desk and wondered if her foolish heart would ever stop yearning for what it couldn't have.

The autumn wore on, filling the wooded valleys with a blaze of glorious colour, the reds and golds brilliant in the late October sunshine.

Jamie was on holiday, a week for half-term, and Emily had a day off on the Tuesday and took him to Watermouth Castle just outside Ilfracombe. They listened to the old musical instruments, marvelled at the kitchen implements of yesteryear, spent a small fortune on the old slot machines and were frightened to death by the animated displays of smugglers and witches.

Out in the garden there were more animated displays, little gnomes all busy about their work, and a playground with a tube slide that Jamie decided was the most wonderful thing in the world.

After he had had a dozen goes Emily managed to drag him away, and she took him then as promised to Putsborough, to have tea with David's parents.

'Can I ride the donkey?' he pleaded, and so David's father took him out into the paddock while Emily swallowed her panic and prayed that Mrs T wouldn't give her the third degree again.

She didn't. Instead she apologised for doing so last time, and then showed Emily a tapestry she was doing to while away the evenings.

'It seems so strange not having the chickens to worry about, and the calves to feed.'

'You must miss the farm.'

'Yes and no. We're happy here, and we see more of David. It was too much for Bill to cope with any longer, anyway, so we had no choice, but we couldn't part with Topsy and when we have children staying in the summer we let them have rides. Bill loves it. He's just a natural grandfather.'

Emily's eyes misted as she watched the old man leading Topsy up the paddock, Jamie's skinny legs dangling down her round sides, a broad grin on his face.

He said something, and David's father turned and laughed, looking so like his son that a pain stabbed through her.

'Oh, Emily—you still love him, don't you?' Mrs T said softly, and she nodded.

'Yes. Yes, I do. It isn't always enough, though, is it?'

'Not when you're too pigheaded to let it be, no,' Mrs T said calmly, and picked up the kettle. 'Time for tea, I think.'

Emily said nothing. How could she make the woman understand? Her rows with David had been bitter and vitriolic, the gulf between them unbreachable. How could she expose Jamie to that, after all he'd been through?

She couldn't, was the simple answer.

With a deep sigh that expressed more than words, she turned away from the window and forced a small smile.

'I'll lay the table, shall I?'

Mrs T said nothing, merely gave a sad, understanding smile and nodded.

They didn't linger over tea, because Mrs Bradley was due to have a few days off and Jamie was going to stay with Philip's parents in Surrey until Saturday. They were leaving early the following morning, and she wanted him to have a good night's sleep.

How she would cope with the emptiness of the cottage she wasn't at all sure. She would have to find herself something to do—perhaps tapestry, like Mrs T, or hire a few hundred videos and tune out the world.

Even so, she would have to sleep, and that was always the worst part. . .

Jenny Wellcome's husband phoned the following day to say that his wife was complaining of double vision and giddiness.

'Brainstem involvement,' David said heavily. 'Oh, hell.'

'Do you think she knew it was coming?' Emily asked.

'Possibly. I don't suppose for a moment she's discussed her living will with him.'

He left to see her, and reported afterwards that she was confused and lacked co-ordination in her hands.

'She's also finding breathing a bit harder. She might have the beginnings of a chest infection. Are you on duty tonight?'

'Yes, I am. Why? Do you want me to look in on her?'

He shrugged. 'I might admit her. I'll go and see her myself again later, and if I think she should come in I'll try and talk her into it, but I imagine she'll resist.'

By five that night she had deteriorated, and David admitted her—albeit reluctantly—to the cottage hospital. Emily went and saw her later, while she was at the hospital for the emergency clinic, and found her frail but stubborn.

'I won't have any antibiotics,' she warned her. 'Don't you let Richard talk you into it. If this is it, fine. I'm ready.'

'You're sure?' Emily asked her.

There was no hesitation. 'Yes, I'm sure. I've had enough. It's time to go.'

Maureen was on duty, and Emily made sure she was aware of Jenny's wishes.

'Oh, hell,' the sister groaned. 'Wait till Richard hears. It'll really hit the fan.'

He did hear—later that evening when he came back to the hospital to say goodnight to his wife and found that she had developed a temperature and was showing signs of a chest infection.

Emily was called to the ward to talk to him, and she phoned David.

'Perhaps you'd like to come and deal with this as he's your patient. He's very upset.'

He was indeed upset, and wanted to talk to his wife about it, but by then she was too ill to concentrate and simply pleaded with him to sit with her. 'Just hold me,' she whispered, and Emily and David watched helplessly as Richard screwed his eyes shut and wrapped his arms tenderly round his wife.

'Please, Jenny, don't leave me,' he murmured brokenly, and they went into the office, leaving the couple with their privacy.

'Are we doing the right thing?' David asked softly.

'Of course. It's what she wants. We have no choice. As the doctor on duty I can't go ahead and treat her against her wishes, knowing how she felt about this at a time when she was perfectly lucid. She's still lucid enough now to change her mind if she wants to, but I don't think she does.'

'Are you absolutely sure? You'll have to live with it on your conscience, Emily.'

'And would that be any harder than living with the knowledge that I'd preserved her, like a vegetable, kept under the most appropriate storage conditions—irradiated if necessary to maintain her freshness?'

She couldn't keep the sarcasm out of her voice, and David gave a sharp sigh.

'Don't fight with me. I'm not arguing against you, just trying to examine all the aspects while there's still time.'

'But there isn't. Time for Jenny ran out years ago. Let her go, David. Please. Give her her dignity.'

He was silent for a long time, then he sighed.

'I'll go and talk to Richard. Carry on with your clinic, I'll take over here.'

'David?'

He turned back to her, his face sober. 'Don't worry, Emily. I'll respect her wishes.'

She felt her shoulders droop with the relief of tension. She had been so afraid that he would disagree and override Jenny's wishes, not only for Jenny's sake but for her own, because that would mean he doubted her professional competence, and for some obscure reason his faith in her judgement meant a great deal to her.

She finished her clinic and went back to the ward, to find Jenny still in much the same state and Richard sitting beside her, holding her hand, his face tortured.

She didn't disturb them, there didn't seem any point, so she asked Maureen to contact her if there was any change and made her way out to her car.

The night was cold, and as she walked out of the hospital she realised that the mist which had hovered over the sea all day had rolled in up the valley, blanketing the land with thick fog.

It was a night like the night on which Sarah had died, and as she drove carefully towards her cottage she found herself panicking. What if she lost her way? Perhaps she already had?

Her headlights just seemed to make the fog worse, and she switched them off, crawling forward by the dim glow of her side-lights and the moon overhead.

The road was muddy, rutted in places where tractors had turned out of the fields, and after a while she realised she was helplessly, hopelessly lost.

Somewhere back there she had made a wrong turning, and her only hope was to turn round and head back to the town.

She stopped the car and got out, checking behind

her, and then carefully reversed off the road into a gateway.

So far so good, she thought, and then as she pulled forward there was a slither and a crash and the car slipped sideways with a sickening lurch.

Stunned, she lay against her door, her lights pointing up into the sky, and let her heart steady. She was all right. She must have misjudged the gateway and turned into a ditch. She would be all right, she would. All she had to do was climb out of the car and walk back towards town. That was all. . .

Turning off the ignition and pocketing the keys, she clambered awkwardly across the tilted seats, and paused. She couldn't hold the door open and climb out, she realised, so she wound down the window and struggled through the little gap, dragging her medical bag behind her. She would need that. She could use the light from her little torch to help see the way—if the battery lasted long enough. . .

She stuffed her fist in her mouth to stifle the sob. Where was she, for heaven's sake? She didn't even know for sure which way the town was!

Downhill, her brain told her. Trembling, her legs still weak from reaction, she turned downhill and slowly, stumbling over the verge from time to time, she began to walk.

She came to a junction and read the sign, then read it again. She was near David's house! Surely this was the lane that led past his cottage! If she could only find it, she would be safe.

Shivering, the cold air seeping through her coat, she began to walk uphill again, away from the town.

Was she right? After a while her brain began to play

tricks on her, and she paused. Downhill was the town. If she was wrong, and this wasn't the lane, she could be walking round in the fog for hours!

Just then there was a teasing breath of wind, and, like a tearing of gauze, the fog lifted for a moment and she saw a cottage, the outside light glowing like a beacon, calling her.

She started to run, her heart pounding, and as she reached the cottage she stumbled and fell against the door.

'David!' she sobbed. 'David!'

The door opened and she fell inside, into his arms.

'Emily? For God's sake, what's happened?'

'I got lost in the fog—I put my car in a ditch and I couldn't find you——'

The sobs refused to be held back, and he scooped her up in his arms and carried her into the sitting-room, flicking on the light as he went.

'Are you all right? Are you hurt?'

She shook her head. 'No—just—oh, I'm being so stupid. . .'

'Shh. You've had a fright. You're OK now, I've got you. You'll be fine. I've got you.'

He settled on to the sofa, still cradling her against his chest, and let her lie there until the sobs died away and her shivering stopped. Then he tipped up her chin, wiped her eyes and smiled.

'Better now?'

She nodded, ashamed of her silliness but unwilling to give up her seat on his lap.

He slid her off, however, and went out, returning with a bottle of brandy and two glasses. 'Here, have

some of this then go and have a hot shower while I get
the fire going. You'll be fine in a bit.'

She nodded, cupping the glass in her palms.

'Drink some,' he told her, and she tipped the glass
and swallowed, choking.

'That's it. OK?'

She coughed again and nodded, her eyes streaming.
'Oh, gosh, that's lovely and warm.'

'How about a shower?'

'Yes—please.'

He led her upstairs to his little bathroom, gave her a
fresh towel and left her alone.

The water was wonderful, piping hot, the stinging
spray warming her chilled flesh and dispelling the fears.
After an age she turned off the taps and stepped out,
wrapping herself in the towel.

'I've put a dressing-gown out for you. Why don't you
just put it on instead of getting dressed?' he said
through the door.

'OK. Thanks.'

She dried herself and then opened the door, to find
a thick, fluffy towelling robe folded neatly on the
landing. There was also a pair of snuggly socks and an
old T-shirt, and she pulled them on, turning over the
sleeves of the robe so that she could see her hands.

Her hair was wet but there was nothing she could do
about it. She borrowed his comb from the shelf over
the basin and got rid of most of the tangles, then went
back down to the sitting-room, supremely conscious of
her nakedness under the robe and T-shirt.

He smiled, and her insides melted. 'OK?'

'Yes—thank you.'

'Come and sit by the fire and finish your drink.'

He drew her down to the rug, pulling her between his legs and easing her back against his chest, his arm round her waist. Then he put the glass in her hand and picked up his.

'Cheers,' he said softly, his voice oddly strained, and she tilted her head to look at him.

'Cheers,' she echoed, but her eyes were on his, her shoulders conscious of the rapid thud of his heart, its beat matching hers.

'The last time we did this it was our wedding night,' he told her softly. 'Do you remember?'

She nodded. 'Yes—yes, I remember.'

He set his glass down, then took hers from her and put it on the table too. Then he shifted slightly so that she lay against his shoulder, and slowly, infinitely carefully, he brought his mouth down against hers.

An anguished moan broke from her lips, and, curling her arms around his neck, she turned herself more fully into his arms.

The kiss was long and slow, thorough, and when he lifted his head she made a tiny sound of pain and tunnelled her hands through his hair, pulling him down to her again.

He groaned, a deep, shattered sound from low in his chest, and his hand slid down her hip and shifted her against him.

'Feel what you do to me,' he grated. 'I want you, Emily—I want you, now, here, tonight.' He drew a ragged breath. 'If that isn't what you want, then for God's sake stop me now.'

She met his eyes, those beautiful, misty grey eyes, so full of love and tenderness and need—years and years of need that found an echo in her heart.

'It's what I want,' she told him softly. 'You're what I want—now—here—tonight. . .'

His breath seemed to lodge in his throat, then with a shattered sigh he drew her down on to the rug and cradled her against his chest.

'I want you so badly—it's been so damn long. . .'

His hands were trembling, nearly as much as hers, and he parted the robe and eased it off her shoulders. The T-shirt followed, pulled slowly over her head to leave her sitting naked in front of him.

He stood and turned off the light, then came back, his hands tracing her skin with a trembling, reverent touch.

'The firelight on your body looks like gold,' he murmured. 'You haven't changed—you look just the same, just as lovely as ever.'

'Take off your clothes,' she whispered. 'Let me see you.'

Standing again, he stripped off the jumper first, then the jeans, tugging them down his long legs and kicking them away.

He straightened, and her breath caught, her heart slamming in her throat like a wild thing.

'David,' she mouthed, and then he was beside her, his arms around her, his body warm and hard against her side.

She slid her hands over the smooth skin of his shoulders, wider now, more solid, and then down, feeling the changes in his ribcage, the depth that maturity had brought. He was truly in his prime now, even more beautiful than in his youth.

His mouth found her breast, teasing the aching peak until she arched against him. She felt the soft puff of his laughter, then he relented and drew her nipple into his mouth, suckling deeply.

She cried out and he lifted his head, his eyes smoky, lazy, teasing. 'Do you like that?'

'You know I do,' she said raggedly.

'And this?'

He slid lower, his tongue trailing fire over the shallow dip of her pelvis, over her hip, down her thigh to the sensitive skin behind her knee, then up again, wreaking havoc with her control, over the soft skin of her inner thigh to her very secret depths.

She sobbed his name, her hands burrowing in his hair, the tension unbearable.

When she could stand it no more he lifted his head, his eyes glittering.

'Now?' he asked her.

'Yes—for God's sake, yes. . .'

The fullness was more than she could stand. The need had gripped her for so long, the wait had been so lonely, and now he was here, with her, inside her. . .

'Now, Emily,' he ground out, the words splintering against her lips. 'Come with me. . .'

The waiting was over.

CHAPTER SEVEN

EMILY woke some time later to the fresh smell of clean sheets, the pillow cool and welcoming beneath her cheek. She was naked, her body warmed by the soft thickness of the down-filled quilt that snuggled round her, and her body ached with the once familiar ache of loving.

In the distance she could hear David's voice as he held a one-sided conversation, and as she lay there she heard his tread on the stairs and he came back into the room.

'Emily?'

'What is it?' she asked softly.

'I have to go out—Jenny Wellcome's going downhill fast. You stay here; I'll be back as soon as I can.'

'What time is it?'

'Nearly four. Go back to sleep.'

She waited till he had left the house, then she slipped out of bed and showered, then went downstairs and made herself a cup of tea.

The fire was still just about alight, and she poked it to life and stared into the flames, thoughtful.

Their loving had been a very beautiful thing, she mused. Her body had remembered his, welcoming it like the prodigal son.

And she had certainly killed the fatted calf. No holding back, no hesitation—it had been beyond her.

Instead she had given him her all, and he had taken it in his hands as if it had been the most treasured gift.

The flames blurred, and she blinked away the tears. She loved him; there was no question of it. And he loved her. If only there was a way she could guarantee their happiness.

Her tea grew cold, and she made another cup and curled up on the rug, her fingers absently smoothing the dogs' ears. They had come in to keep her company, and now lay, one each side, their heads on her lap.

'Soppy great things,' she scolded fondly, and their tails thumped in response. She wondered how Jamie was getting on with his grandparents. After he came back she planned to get him a puppy from the RSPCA. They had a litter of Labrador crosses, too young yet to leave their mother, but she had chosen a little black bitch with a white star on her chest and the sweetest, softest nose she had ever felt.

She wondered how the dog would get on with David's two—not that it mattered, she told herself, because they wouldn't ever need to be together.

An ache started, deep in her heart, and she bit her lip and wondered how she could be so foolish.

What was she doing, sitting here in his dressing-gown with the smell of his body warm about her, waiting for him to return? She must have been mad to let him love her last night, crazy to allow her body to override her common sense.

Belatedly she thought about Jenny Wellcome and wondered if she was still alive and if she would see the dawn.

Perhaps they should take love where they found it, because there might not be a tomorrow. For Sarah and

Philip, at least, there would be no more tomorrows.
She might have died herself last night if the ditch had
been deeper or full of water.

She thought of Richard, worried about his wife,
about the farm, about Ann. She thought of Neil Blake
and the wife who no longer loved him, and their child
used as a weapon in their marriage.

And she thought again of Jenny, who might not see
the dawn.

It made her problems seem very trivial.

David returned shortly before seven.

She was still sitting on the floor, and as the dogs
leapt up to greet him she climbed stiffly to her feet.

'Jenny?' she asked, but she could see the answer on
his face.

'She died shortly after I got there. I've been with
Richard.'

'How is he?'

'Wrecked. I've taken him home and made him a
drink and put him to bed with a sedative, but he's very
shocked. His mother was coming over, and the man
who does the milking was already there. He'll keep an
eye on him.'

He gave a harsh sigh and rubbed his hand over his
eyes.

'I need a hug,' he told her gruffly, and she went
unquestioning into his arms.

'Come back to bed,' she coaxed.

He followed her, his hand in hers, and their loving
was wild and tender and touched with fear.

Afterwards he held her close, his heart beating
beneath her ear.

'I couldn't bear to lose you again,' David whispered. His voice was raw, his hands trembling as they smoothed her shoulders. 'Stay with me, Emily. Marry me—let me love you.'

She turned her face into his shoulder, her heart aching.

'David, I daren't. What about Jamie? He's been through so much. What if things go wrong again? What if we start to fight?'

'We won't,' he promised, but she didn't believe him. They were too different, too opinionated, both of them, to offer such assurances.

'We will. And when we do it will tear him apart.'

He sighed. 'You won't even give us a chance.'

'We had a chance, David. We blew it.'

'We were kids. We didn't know about compromise. We just took, and if it wasn't there we sulked.'

He smoothed her hair, his hand warm and gentle against her head. 'I love you, Emily. You mean everything to me. I'd cut my tongue out before I lost you again because of anything I'd said to hurt you.'

She squeezed her eyes tight shut. 'David, please——' Her voice broke and she turned her face into his shoulder. 'It isn't possible.'

'It could be,' he told her, his voice harsher now. 'We might have a chance, only you won't even dare to try. Damn, Emily, what have we got to lose?'

'But Jamie——'

'To hell with Jamie—leave him out of this.'

'But I can't! That's just it, David—I can't leave him out!' She struggled into a sitting position and turned to face him, her eyes wide with pain. 'He's had enough,' she said with emphasis. 'He can't take any more change, any more trauma. I *can't* forget him.'

He sat up, dragging the quilt up over his chest and folding his arms over it like a shield.

'I didn't mean like that——'

She snorted. 'How else, for God's sake?'

'I just meant now, for a while, until we see——'

'You're yelling at me.'

His mouth opened, then clamped shut into a grim line. 'I'm sorry,' he muttered. 'I just meant—give us a chance, without worrying about Jamie. Give us some time alone, away from him, to see if what we have can be made to work. I don't want him hurt any more than you do, but if our marriage could be made to work, if we could only find a way to live together in harmony— wouldn't that be better for him—to live in a real family, with other children, rather than with two lonely widows?'

Her shoulders drooped. He was right, of course, but she was so afraid. What if it didn't work? Was it really Jamie she was trying to protect? Or herself?

'Emily?'

She took a steadying breath and met his eyes.

'OK. We'll give it a try—find some time on our own, see if we can make it work.'

His eyes blurred and filled. 'Thank you,' he breathed, and then he drew her into his arms. 'Thank you,' he said again, his voice gruff with emotion, and then he laid his lips against hers.

It wasn't really a kiss, she thought—more like a prayer.

A prayer for peace. . .

*   *   *

The surgery was subdued that day. Jenny Wellcome's death was felt keenly by all the residents of the town where she had been born and raised, and it was the first and last topic on everybody's lips.

'Poor Jenny,' they all said.

'Poor Richard,' some said.

Ann Blake came in for her share of flak. It seemed their affair was more widely known about than had been appreciated, and it certainly didn't go down well, especially with the women.

Emily kept out of it, making non-committal noises if a patient brought up the subject, and bit by bit the day was eroded.

After evening surgery David came in to tell her that her car had been pulled out of the ditch and was in the local body-repair shop where it would be fixed by tomorrow.

'I'll drive you home,' he told her. 'Your place or mine?'

Her heart thumped. 'Mine, please. I need a change of clothes and a shower, at least.'

'OK. We'll start with that. I have to go out and see Richard Wellcome later, and I have to see to the dogs, so perhaps we'll adjourn to my cottage after you've picked up some things for you, if that's all right?'

'Fine.'

His smile was warm and filled with tenderness. 'Don't worry, darling,' he said softly. 'We'll be all right. Just give it time.'

They had a lovely evening. They called in briefly to collect her things, then went back and took the dogs for a quick stroll down the lane before lighting the fire and making a cup of tea. After they had drunk it David went to see Richard and she fossicked about in the freezer for something to eat.

By the time he returned the house was redolent with the scent of herbs and wine, the chicken casserole simmering gently on the Aga.

'Oh, wow, that smells good.'

'You've got all the ingredients, but I bet you never put them together.'

He wrinkled his nose. 'I always mean to, but I somehow never get round to it.' He tugged her gently into his arms and nuzzled her nose against his. 'Mmm. You feel good.' His hips shifted against hers, and desire widened her eyes.

'David. . .' She laughed raggedly, and he smiled and shifted again.

'Oh, yes—does that feel good?'

'You know it does.'

'So tell me. Communicate. That's where we went wrong, darling. We never bothered to communicate except in bed.'

Her face lost its sparkle. 'Maybe because that's all there was to our marriage.'

'Oh, no.' He released her and stood back. 'No, Emily, you're wrong. There was much more than that. We just never bothered to look for it. That's why I want to try again, to see if we can find the good things and bring them to life, instead of just going through the motions.'

'Once more, with feeling?' she said wryly.

'Exactly.'

She held out her arms. 'Oh, David—I do so hope you're right.'

'I am. Trust me. Now, where were we?'

His hips lifted against hers and pushed her back against the worktop. She was wearing a denim skirt that fastened with press-studs down the front. With a quick tug he undid it from hem to waist, sliding his hand inside along the length of her naked thigh.

'I want you,' he said gruffly.

'Here? Now?'

'Here. Now.'

The air shivered with the rasp of his zip, and then they were joined, their bodies locked together, their mouths meshed in a desperate kiss.

Suddenly her legs gave as wave after wave of ecstasy pounded her body.

'David,' she sobbed, and she felt him stiffen and drive into her one last time.

'My God, woman—we haven't even closed the curtains,' he muttered gruffly, and, easing away from her, he reached behind her and twitched the curtains shut.

She started to laugh, bubbles of hysteria mounting up inside her like champagne, flowing over and caressing him.

'You're a crazy woman, do you know that? I love you.'

'I love you, too.'

He was absolutely still, then his eyes welled and he tugged her back into his arms. 'Thank God,' he said gruffly. 'Now let's eat; I'm starving.'

The rest of the week passed in a haze of sensuous langour. Emily's car was returned, and they made sure it was outside her cottage at night even though they spent most of the time at his.

The locals loved a scandal, and Richard Wellcome and Ann Blake were getting to be old news.

On Saturday afternoon Jamie and Mrs Bradley returned, their faces beaming, and it was clear that they'd both had a wonderful time.

Mrs Bradley's daughter had recently had another baby, and the motherly woman had obviously spent the past three days thoroughly enjoying being a grandmother.

As for Jamie, Philip's parents had probably spoiled him to death but he seemed to be thriving on it.

'We went to the cinema,' he told her, 'and Grandad took me to the airport and we watched the planes take off and land——Emmy, can I be a pilot when I grow up?'

'I expect so,' she said fondly, and hugged him. 'Would you like that?'

He nodded furiously. 'The planes are t'rrific—huge, and all shiny.' He glanced out of the window as if to assure himself that there really wasn't room to park one in the garden, and Emily had to school her expression.

'Grandad said Daddy used to have a plane, but I don't 'member it.'

'No, it was a long time ago. He used to fly a little plane.'

'Is it mine now?'

'No, darling, it was sold.'

'Oh.' He looked wistful. 'We could have kept it for me to learn on.'

She hugged him. 'You can have a new one when you're old enough, if you still want to. You might not.'

'I will,' he assured her, his eyes like saucers, and she had the distinct feeling he might. Philip had loved flying, and he had been very sad the day the plane was sold.

'There's no point in keeping it; I shan't ever fly again,' he'd said heavily, but it had hurt him none the less. As Emily looked at his son now, she could see the same wistful look in Jamie's eyes.

Yes, there was a lot of his father in him. Philip would have been very proud, and so would Sarah.

The huge weight of her responsibility seemed to settle on Emily's shoulders then. Raising someone else's child was a mammoth undertaking, there was no doubt.

Maybe she had misjudged herself. What if she failed in her task and let them all down—Sarah, Philip and little Jamie? What if she allowed her need for David to cloud her judgement over Jamie's well-being?

'Oh, God, help me to do the right thing for him,' she whispered.

'Did you say something, Emmy?'

She looked down at the trusting little face turned up to hers and smiled. 'Nothing important. How about some supper?' she suggested.

'Can I have beans on toast with cheese?'

'Yes.'

'Goodie. Now?'

'Yes, now.'

She let him tug her into the kitchen, and resolved to put David out of her mind. While she was with him, she would think of him. Now, though, she was with Jamie, and she would give him the attention he needed and deserved.

* * *

Jenny Wellcome's funeral took place on the first Wednesday in November. It was a brilliant, beautiful day, unseasonally warm, and the clear air rang loud with the tolling of the church bell.

Emily didn't go to the funeral—she didn't feel it was her place—but David went and sat at the back of the church.

'How was Richard?' she asked him when he returned to the surgery.

'Grim. I'm worried about him.'

'Do you think he needs psychiatric support?'

'Probably. At the very least he needs bereavement counselling. I imagine he's a seething mass of guilt and self-recrimination. I'll go and see him later.'

But later he was busy, called out to an elderly lady who had fallen and refused to go into Barnstaple to have her hip pinned. He phoned Emily and asked her if she could pop in on Richard on her way home, as he was going to be held up for some time, and so after she had finished her surgery she made her way up the valley to the Wellcomes' farm.

A car passed her on the way down, and she thought she recognised the driver as Ann Blake. She looked upset, and Emily wondered if she'd been to see Richard.

Not, perhaps, the most opportune timing—or maybe it was.

She found him in the farm office next to the back door, his feet on the desk, his head sunk forward on his chest.

He had been drinking, and Emily noticed a hand-written letter lying on the pile of paperwork.

She hesitated in the doorway. 'Can I come in?' she asked.

He looked up, his eyes unfocused, and his shoulder shifted slightly.

She took it for assent and tipped a ginger cat off the chair by the window, sitting down and eyeing Richard thoughtfully.

He looked grim. His eyes were red-rimmed, his face was pale, and there was a bleak set to his mouth.

'Are you all right?' she asked him gently.

He gave a short grunt of laughter. 'Oh, fine, Dr Thompson—just dandy.' He sighed and lifted a bottle off the floor beside him, tipping it back and swigging deeply. 'I buried my wife today, Doctor—how the hell do you think I feel?'

'Very sad, I would imagine. Perhaps angry with her for dying, guilty for still being alive yourself.'

He laughed again. 'Guilty?' He dropped his feet to the floor and swung round to face her. 'Did you see Ann leaving?'

'I thought it was her. She looked upset.'

'I just told her it was over.'

'Ah.'

The ginger cat rubbed against Emily's legs and she bent and stroked it absently.

'She knew.'

'Your wife?'

'Knew all about it—had from the beginning, apparently. Said she understood.' Again, the bitter laugh. 'Damned if I did. Ann just filled a need. I never loved her—not like she loved me. I knew it was wrong, but it seemed to help me cope. I still loved Jenny—still do——' His voice cracked, and he closed his eyes briefly. When he opened them, his voice sounded stronger.

'The farm will have to go, of course, to pay the debts. Funny, I would have moved heaven and earth to save it while she was alive, but it doesn't seem to matter now. They can sell it, do what they like with it. It won't matter to me.'

His gaze switched to her, focusing for the first time.

'I'll be all right, Dr Thompson. Don't you worry about me. I'll be fine.'

She stood up and shook his hand. 'Call if you need us,' she told him, and then she left.

As she walked past the window she glanced in at him and saw his eyes drop to the paper on the desk.

A note from his wife?

Quite possibly.

She left him alone with his grief.

The phone rang at six the next morning. It was David.

'Could you come up to the Wellcomes' farm, Emily?'

She was still groggy with sleep, and rubbed her eyes as she hitched up the bed and propped herself on the pillow.

'What, now?' she mumbled.

'I'm afraid so. The police would like to speak to you.'

She was wide awake now.

'Police?' she said, filled with foreboding.

'Richard Wellcome shot himself last night.'

'Oh, my God—is he dead?'

There was a slight pause. 'Yes—extremely. Could you come? They want to talk to you before they move the body.'

She woke Mrs Bradley, explained the situation and quickly pulled on some clothes. She would come back and shower later. Just now, though, she wanted to get up to the farm and find out what had happened.

The farmyard was littered with vehicles when she arrived—police cars, an ambulance, David's car and another she didn't recognise that turned out to belong to the milker, the man who had found Richard at five-thirty that morning.

She went into the office and winced.

'A shotgun in the mouth isn't a very tidy way of doing away with yourself,' the police officer said apologetically. 'I wonder, Dr Thompson, if you can confirm that he was the man you spoke to last night?'

'Yes—yes, of course he is.' She turned her head away from the grisly sight and sought David's eyes. 'What happened?'

'The milker found him this morning. It seems likely that you were the last person who saw him alive— unless Ann Blake was here after you?'

'She'd been,' Emily confirmed. 'I passed her going the other way. She looked upset—I don't know if it's relevant but they'd been having an affair.'

'So I understand,' the policeman said. 'We'll be talking to Mrs Blake later. Have you any idea of the content of their meeting?'

'He told me he'd just ended their relationship.'

'Really?' David sounded surprised.

'Really. He said he didn't love her—I think he'd just discovered that Jenny knew all about their affair, and possibly he felt guilty. There was a letter on the desk, handwritten on blue paper.'

'This one?' The policeman held up a blood-splattered piece of paper sealed in a plastic folder.

'That looks like it.'

'You'd better read it—see if it sheds any light for you on his behaviour.'

She ran her eye over it. It was tender, understanding and very much the way Jenny had spoken of Richard in their conversation back in September. It held no surprises for Emily, but for Richard it might well have done.

'He didn't realise she knew—he told me that. Otherwise I don't think there's anything there. He was worried about the farm—said he would have moved heaven and earth to save it when she was alive, but it didn't matter now. He said something odd, actually. He said they could sell it, whoever "they" are. The executors, I suppose. God, I should have realised—he told me to go. Said he'd be all right. I told him to phone if he needed us.'

She handed the note back to the policeman. 'Did he leave a note himself? Anything to indicate why he did it?'

The man shook his head. 'Not that we can find. He'd been drinking.'

'Yes, he was drinking while I was here.'

He asked her to go over the whole content of their conversation the previous evening, and she did so, twice. Finally satisfied that he had all the information he was likely to get from her, he dismissed them and she and David went out into the yard.

She took a great, steadying gulp of fresh air and closed her eyes.

'Are you all right?'

She nodded. 'Not a pretty sight.'

'No. I'm sorry they called you.'

'It's OK. David, I should have done something last night. I should have realised he was a danger to himself. He was too calm.'

'You can't be clairvoyant, Emily. Perhaps this is for the best.'

'How can you say that? The man's life has just been thrown away and you say it's for the best? Where's your compassion?'

'Where's yours? Like Jenny, he'd reached the end of his rope, but unlike Jenny he didn't have the easy way at his disposal. Whatever, it's done now and flagellating yourself won't do any good.'

'I still think you're wrong,' she said stubbornly. 'I should have done something more to help him. Maybe letting Jenny die was the wrong thing to do.'

'You had no choice over that.'

She turned to face him. 'Didn't I? I think we both did—and I think somewhere along the line we both made the wrong decision.'

CHAPTER EIGHT

EMILY's doubts about her handling of Richard and Jenny Wellcome persisted, despite all that Laurence Allen said to her in the long case-conference she had with him after the tragic events of that week.

He supported her actions entirely, but she was still racked by guilt, and David's dismissal of her worries was hurtful.

It caused a rift between them, and even led to a bitter row one evening in the surgery.

He found her sitting at her desk long after her last patient had left, and came in.

'Come on, Emily. Buck up and come and have a drink. You need cheering up.'

She shook her head. 'No—I don't want a drink.'

'No, you want to turn the clock back and you can't. You did the right thing, Emily.'

'I don't think so.' She stood up and snapped her bag shut, lifting it on to the desk and leaning on it. 'I think I should have tried to talk Jenny out of her living will, and I think I should have insisted that she discuss it with Richard before it went on her records, and I think I should have admitted him to hospital the night he killed himself because I should have realised he was unstable.'

'He wasn't.'

'He was! And I didn't realise, because my professional judgement was at fault!'

135

David snorted. 'Not nearly as at fault as it was when you put Clare Remington on the Pill!'

'Oh, brilliant! What was I supposed to do, let her get pregnant? She was already sleeping with him!'

'Don't yell—there are still people in the building.'

'So what?' she snapped, but she lowered her voice none the less. 'David, I put her on the Pill because the consequences of not doing so were predictable and more potentially harmful than not doing so.'

'I agree—but the shades of grey in that are much more pronounced than in the Wellcomes' case.'

'No, they are not! There are no shades of grey where Clare is concerned, none at all. Having sex without contraception is foolish in the extreme——'

'So what have we been doing?'

She froze. 'Oh, God.'

'Quite.' He turned away. 'Just remember—what Jenny Wellcome wanted to do was within the law. What Clare Remington and her boyfriend are doing is not.'

It was a chilling thought—nearly as chilling as the one which followed.

She could be pregnant.

As the days went by, her fears turned to reality, and then a slow, warm joy that filled her as surely as David's child would do in the months to come.

She was pregnant, the baby conceived within that first hectic twenty-four hours after her crash.

At first she was horrified, but then she thought it would make no difference. She had Mrs Bradley and Jamie, anyway—another child would fit neatly into the puzzle, with or without its father.

She wouldn't deny him access, of course—she couldn't even consider anything so cruel—but whether they ended up together or not was almost immaterial. She would have her child—David's child—after all. She decided not to tell him, although it was difficult to hide her happiness.

Clare Remington came to her for a check-up and seemed well and settled nicely on the Pill. 'It's great,' she told Emily. 'There's a hole in my mattress—I hide them in there and no one knows.'

Emily, who still wished the girl would discuss it with her parents, tried once again to persuade her, but without luck. Physically, though, the girl was well and suffering from no side-effects, and so she was unable to fault her decision on medical grounds.

Ethics she tried not to think about.

They were busy in the hospital as the winter drew on, with flu epidemics and tummy bugs and the usual falls on slippery paths.

Harry Orr, the man with the recurrent dislocation of the shoulder, came in yet again to Casualty at the hospital. This time Emily was on duty on her own, and, not being strong enough to return the arm to its socket the way Laurence had, she laid him down on his front and supported his arm for him, gradually allowing it to hang until it was totally supported on the joint. Then she pulled gently and with a sloppy click it slid back into place.

'Ooo, damn,' he muttered, and lay there for a moment, the arm dangling.

'You know, Mr Orr, you really should have that seen to. You could have an operation to tighten the supporting structures so that such frequent dislocation couldn't happen. Wouldn't you like that?'

'Like the result—not so sure about the op,' he said with a laugh, and carefully, supporting his arm in his other hand, he swung himself into a sitting position. 'Damn, that's sore.'

'I'm sure it is—and just as sure that you need to get something done about it. You'll get arthritis in it if you let it go on like this, and one day you might get severe nerve damage.'

'I dare say,' he mumbled. 'Maureen on?'

'No, there's a staff nurse on. Shall I get her to put it in a sling for you?'

'If you wouldn't mind,' he said wearily. 'Suppose I ought to be thinking about this op.'

'I think you should. Come and see me if you decide you want to go ahead—we can always get you an appointment with the orthopaedic surgeon while you consider it.'

'Mmm.'

She left him sitting there, his face thoughtful, and asked the staff nurse to attend to him while she dealt with the other patients.

She was unsurprised when he came to see her the following week.

'Decided to see the surgeon,' he told her. 'Oh, and the missus sent this for you.' He set a large white pot on the table.

More clotted cream, the thought of which turned her stomach, which was just getting delicate.

'Thank you,' she said, forcing a smile. 'My son will be thrilled.'

'You mind you have some, too. Put a little meat on those bones. You lost weight?'

'Only a little—it's you. You keep me so busy rushing round putting your arm back.'

He winked. 'Not the way I hear it.'

'Pardon?'

'The way I hear it, you're giving that Dr Trevellyan the run-around, like you did before all those years ago.'

Emily was startled. 'What?' she whispered.

'Oh, don't worry, pet. We know things went wrong and you got married again. No one holds it against you. It's just that Dr Trevellyan's very popular about these parts, and we'd all like to see him marry again. His own wife'd be even better.'

Emily sat back in her chair and put her pen down. 'Is it common knowledge?' she asked quietly.

'Lord knows. I heard it from George up at the Bull. He hasn't been here long enough to remember, but there are those in there—regulars, you know—who remember you from your honeymoon. Old friend of Sarah's, weren't you? She and Philip were popular in these parts. Gather you married him and now you've got the lad. Big responsibility, that.'

Emily was amazed by the extent of his knowledge— and by the fact that she had let him discuss her in this open way without any attempt to halt him.

She opened her mouth to speak, but he held up his hand.

'I shan't spread it, my love. Only them as knows already will know. I'll see to it. Don't want lots of nasty gossip spreading, do we? Now, about this blasted arm of mine. . .'

* * *

Emily told David, but he wasn't surprised. 'Harry knows most things worth knowing. If he says it'll go no further, it won't.'

He pushed her door shut and came over to where she was sitting at her desk.

'How about a drink tonight? We haven't spent any time alone together for weeks.'

'I didn't think you wanted to,' she said bitterly. 'You don't seem to trust my judgement.'

'I trust your judgement,' he said, surprised. 'It's you that has trouble with it.' He sighed. 'Emily, forget our ethical differences. What about us?'

'Aren't they the same thing?'

'No. Surely we can agree to differ about work.'

'On something so fundamental? It's not quite like the difference between prescribing Amoxil or Ciproxen for a chest infection!'

His mouth tipped into a wry smile. 'It is—in a way. We're both qualified, we make valued judgements. Who's to say if we're right or wrong? Being right most of the time is what it's about.'

'No,' she argued. 'Being right all the time is what it's about.'

He laughed. 'Well, lady, I'm not vain enough to imagine I ever could be.'

'You've changed, then. There was a time when you would never admit you were wrong.'

Their eyes locked.

'I have changed. I keep telling you that. I just wish you'd believe me.'

'I wish I dared.'

'Come home with me tonight. I need you.'

'I can't. Mrs Bradley's got the evening off.'

'Then let me come and sit and watch television with you and have a cup of coffee by the fire.'

'You'd be content with that?'

He smiled. 'I'd have to be. Well, I might try and sneak the odd kiss.'

She laughed. 'All right, but come at eight-thirty, after Jamie's safely in bed. Oh, and there's a surprise.'

'A surprise? What sort of surprise?'

She thought of the puppy, probably curled up fast asleep beside Jamie as they spoke. 'You'll see.'

He arrived just before eight-thirty—and just as Beauty, the puppy, piddled on the sitting-room floor.

'Oh, Beauty! Oh, darling, not now!' Emily wailed, and, scooping her up, she went to the door. 'Here, hold this; she's just peed.'

'Wha——? Hello, sweetheart. Aren't you lovely?'

The puppy decided he was dirty and washed him thoroughly while Emily blotted the carpet.

'It's bound to stain,' she groaned.

'No, it won't. She's gorgeous; when did you get her?'

'Tuesday—I've been dying to show her to you.'

His look was reproachful. 'You only had to ask.'

'I didn't like to. I thought——'

'What?'

She shrugged. 'I don't know. We seemed to be fighting again.'

He shook his head and sat down, pulling her down beside him. 'No, we weren't fighting, we were disagreeing, and the only reason it seemed as if it was all we were doing is because it's been the only communication we've had. As soon as we disagree about anything, we cut off all other lines of communication. We always did.'

She slumped against his side, her finger tracing the wave in Beauty's fur. 'We did, didn't we?'

'We should stop—make ourselves talk about anything and everything, try and get to know each other instead of assuming. We've both changed. Time does that to people.'

He smoothed her hair back from her face and leant across, dropping a light kiss on her lips. 'I love you. Remember that when you get cross with me, when things go wrong and we can't seem to find a way out.'

'I love you, too,' she told him softly. 'I try and remember, but there are times when other things seem more important.'

'No. They aren't more important. They just tend to overwhelm it.'

She nodded, and scooped the puppy off his lap. 'Come on, nuisance—you need to go in the garden for a minute and then have a sleep. You're still a baby.'

He followed her out to the kitchen and watched as she put the puppy out. 'Coffee?' she asked as she washed her hands.

'Mmm, lovely—can I do it?'

She laughed. 'Probably not. You make everybody's thick and black like yours. I'll do it.'

He pulled a face and tugged her into his arms. 'Critical witch, aren't you? I want you to myself.'

'Mmm,' she murmured.

'When?'

'Tomorrow?'

He nodded. 'That'll do, I suppose.'

A sharp yap from the back door drew them apart, David to let the dog in, Emily to make the coffee.

As they went back into the sitting-room, David told

her that Joe Hardwill had been discharged from the
North Devon General to the cottage hospital.

'He's still on crutches and very weak, and still
coughing like crazy, but he's making progress.'

'I'm on duty there tomorrow—I'll go and introduce
myself.'

'He'll be delighted. I told him you might come—he
said he'd have to find his comb. I ought to warn you, I
think he probably knows about us. At least a certain
amount.'

'Doesn't everybody?' she said with a sigh.

'We could always satisfy their urge for romance.'

She sighed again, this time more heavily.

'Sorry, I'm pushing you.'

His face was tight, his eyes closed, and she felt guilty
for what she was doing to him. Still, until she was
sure—and at the moment she was far from sure—there
was no point in discussing it any further.

He went at eleven, after a kiss that left them both
hot and aching for more.

'Till tomorrow,' he said, and his words throbbed
with promise.

'Mr Hardwill? I'm Dr Thompson.'

The old man in the chair on the balcony turned
towards her, bright, curious eyes searching her face.

'Well, there's a sight for sore eyes,' he said slowly.
His voice was scratchy, and he coughed at the end,
pressing his hand against his ribs. 'Oh, damn cough.'

'Well, it should improve now you've given up
smoking.'

The beady eyes twinkled. 'Who told you that
malarky?'

She smiled. 'Well, almost. I don't imagine you get much past Maureen Whitaker.'

'That old battleaxe! Have to wait till she's off duty before they can sneak me any in. I hide them.'

'Do you?' she said, playing along with him. 'Where?'

He laughed, a rusty cackle that turned into a racking cough. 'That'd be telling,' he said finally.

'Hmm. You're a fool to yourself, you know. You nearly went—they almost lost you after your operation.'

He made a dismissive noise. 'Going to look at my leg?' he asked.

'No. I gather it's doing well, and Dr Trevellyan looked at it yesterday. I'm sure it hasn't changed.'

'Told you all about it, did he?' the old man asked, a sly note creeping into his voice. 'Over dinner, perhaps?'

She schooled her smile. 'Over coffee, actually. If you give me your cigarettes, I'll tell you all about it.'

He chuckled. 'You doctors've got more tricks than a magician's rabbit. I'll hang on to the fags, thank you, my dear.'

She smiled. 'Oh, well, it was worth a try.'

She left him chuckling, and checked the other patients on the wards before heading back to the surgery.

She had a family planning clinic that afternoon, and one of her patients was Amy Richardson.

'Hi,' Amy said, a smile across her pretty face.

'Hello. How's the baby?'

'Lovely. He's nine weeks now, and I think we ought to do something about contraception. Jeremy wants a vasectomy, but I'm not sure.'

'Isn't five enough?' Emily asked her. 'Just thinking about all that washing and cooking gives me the shivers.'

Amy smiled. 'I have help. It's just—when the baby gets to about a year, I get this ache—sort of a crazy, biological bomb—do you know what I mean?'

Emily nodded. She did, only too well.

'I just have to have another baby. Do you know what it's like to feel a baby grow inside you, to know that this week it's got fingers and toes, this week eyelashes——? You feel it move, like a butterfly, then a team of fullbacks——' She laughed. 'Then they arrive, small and defenceless, and all your energy is focused in on them, on caring for them, watching them grow. Then suddenly they can walk and talk, and bang—off goes the bomb again.'

Emily closed her eyes briefly. Oh, she knew so clearly what the woman was talking about. Under cover of her desk, her hand slid across and cradled her child, buried deep in her pelvis, still too tiny to be noticeable but there, a powerful presence for all that.

'I think I understand,' she said quietly. 'The thing is, when do you stop? Obviously economic and social decisions have to be made, but there are medical decisions too. How well is your body taking the demands of so many pregnancies?'

'Oh, fine. I'm religious about my pelvic floor exercises, and we've got a swimming-pool that I use every day. Jeremy freaks a bit about all the school fees, but we aren't exactly strapped for cash. He's a writer, a very successful one—political bestsellers. He's had one televised as a series, and they want a sequel.'

'He said you were broke,' Emily reminded her with a smile.

'Oh, he fusses. He'd just had a tax demand. The next advance paid it with tons left. Trust me, money isn't a problem, and nor is my body.'

'You could have a coil.'

'That's how we had David.'

'Ah. Well, a cap?'

'That was Julian.'

Emily rolled her eyes. 'The Pill?'

'I can't take it. I forget. It isn't medical, it's just that I'm useless. That's how we had Lucy. I don't suppose— I read about these implants. They last five years or something.'

'Norplant. Yes. They're like little rods of contraceptive inserted under the skin of your upper arm, and they prevent pregnancy just like the Pill—only more effectively, if you forget to take it.'

Amy laughed. 'What about if we decided we wanted another? I mean, I really don't think we do, when I'm being sensible, but if we did?'

'You can have it removed, and fertility is quickly restored.'

'Can you do it?'

'Yes. Well, I've done the training, but I haven't done one recently. Perhaps one of the other partners has.'

'Is it difficult?'

'Oh, no. You make a tiny incision, about two millimetres long, and push the rods in under the skin. They're very tiny. The whole thing is done under local anaesthetic and takes about twenty minutes.'

'Can I go for it?'

Emily nodded. 'I don't see why not. We may not

have any stocks here in the dispensary, but we should be able to get it fairly quickly. In the meantime, what are you using?'

'Condoms.' She wrinkled her nose, and Emily smiled.

'It's better than getting pregnant again so quickly. Can I ring you?'

'Sure. You should have my number.'

Emily checked it and then promised to get on to it straight away.

She tackled Laurence over tea.

'Norplant? Yes, we can get it. Takes about twenty-four hours to come. Who wants it?'

'Amy Richardson.'

He laughed. 'Bit long-term for her, isn't it?'

Emily grinned. 'I think she's trying to buck the habit—unlike Joe Hardwill. David, he's still smoking.'

David smiled lazily. 'What did you expect? Devious old bugger. I wonder where he hides them?'

'I tried to bribe him into telling me, but he wouldn't play.'

David chuckled. 'Surprise, surprise. Did he embarrass you?'

She shook her head. 'No, I was expecting it. He said I was a sight for sore eyes.'

'And so you are, my dear,' Laurence said, getting to his feet with a sigh. '"Once more unto the breach, dear friends"—oh, that reminds me, Mr Remington's coming to see me tonight. From what Sue said, I think you'd better stand by, Emily. Looks like he's found out about his daughter.'

* * *

Nigel Remington was a big man—tall, solid and very, very angry. He insisted on Emily's being present at the consultation, as well as Laurence, the senior partner, and Clare, the cause of all the trouble.

His wife, pale, tired and obviously upset, hovered by his side. Clare stood awkwardly in the corner, her face sulky, her eyes red-rimmed.

'I want an inquiry,' her father said furiously, 'into how a fifteen-year-old girl came to be prescribed a dangerous drug without her parents' knowledge or consent. You should be struck off! What did you think you were playing at?' he demanded, turning to Emily.

'I wasn't playing at anything, Mr Remington,' she told him as calmly as she could. 'I took a very detailed history, we spent a great deal of time discussing it and in the end I did what I considered to be the right thing for Clare, in my professional judgement.'

'Your what?' The man snorted. 'Let me tell you, Dr Thompson, there's nothing professional about your judgement, though what one can expect from a doctor with your sort of moral standards is difficult to anticipate.'

Emily drew in a sharp breath. 'I beg your pardon?'

'Don't pretend not to know what I'm talking about— unless you'd like me to elaborate in front of Clare?'

'I think,' Laruence said, his voice tight with anger, 'that we are rather getting off the point. The point is, your daughter, for whatever reason, sought contraceptive advice *after* she had embarked on a sexual relationship. In my opinion Dr Thompson did only what I or any other of my partners would have done in the same circumstances. She took steps to ensure that the girl was protected from the effects of an unwanted teenage pregnancy—a pregnancy that I'm sure you would have found a great deal more offensive than the alternative.'

The man's cheeks were mottled with rage, but he contained it. 'She should have been advised against the relationship. She should have been given moral advice to protect her from the evils of the flesh——'

'I quite agree,' Emily butted in. 'And as I see it that advice is the province of the parents. Where were you when she needed to talk to you?'

'We were there,' he said furiously.

'Yes—stuck up on your high horse, too busy stuffing the Bible down my throat to bother to listen to what I had to say!' Clare cut in. 'Well, now you know! I'm sleeping with Colin, I love him, and as soon as I'm sixteen we'll get married!'

'Over my dead body!' her father roared.

'It can be arranged,' Clare muttered under her breath, but her father heard her and raised his hand as if to strike her.

Emily stepped quickly between them.

'I shouldn't,' she said calmly.

Slowly, inch by inch, his hand fell. His eyes burned into Emily's, the hatred and fervour in them terrifying.

'You haven't heard the last of this,' he said, and the volume of anger bottled up behind his words chilled Emily to the bone.

He ushered his wife and daughter out, and Emily sank down on to a chair and looked helplessly at Laurence.

'What a monster,' she said, her voice trembling.

'Isn't he just? Don't worry, Emily, I'm behind you. He can't touch you. I've looked at the notes, and they're very thorough and comprehensive. You covered everything a judge might want to consider.'

The mention of a judge made Emily's blood run cold. She was, after all, only on probation. If things got messy, perhaps they wouldn't want her to stay on.

'You look worried.'

She met his eyes. 'Laurence, do you trust my professional judgement?'

'Of course.'

'What about the Wellcomes?'

He shrugged. 'That was tricky. David should have gone to see him that evening. He knew he was upset.'

'He asked me to go. He trusted me to make the right decisions about his state of mind and treatment.'

'And you don't think you did.' It wasn't a question.

'Do you?'

'On balance, no, but that's with the twenty-twenty vision of hindsight. However, there is a lot of evidence to suggest he would have done it some other time, if not that night. Let's face it, he had precious little left to live for. No, Emily, you did the right thing, both with Jenny and with Richard. And, I believe, with Clare.'

He rested a large, comforting hand on her shoulder. 'Don't worry. It'll all come out in the wash.'

She dredged up a smile and left, tidying up a few things on her desk before heading for home.

Jamie was tucking into chicken pie, peas and carrots when she arrived, and she smiled and kissed him on the forehead.

'Hello, darling. Good day at school?'

'Mmm. I'm a shepherd in the Nativity play. I wanted to be a king, but there weren't enough crowns and besides, I've got a sheepdog. Emmy, can I take Beauty with me to do the play?'

'Oh, darling—she might piddle on the stage.'

He giggled. 'Yes, she might. I know, you can video it and we can show her.'

'I'll do that,' she promised, and then straightened up. 'I must go and get changed; David's taking me out for supper tonight.'

'Can I come?'

She looked down at the bright, eager face and her heart sank. 'Not this time, sweetheart. Maybe another day—perhaps at the weekend.'

'This weekend?'

'No, I'm on duty.'

His face fell. 'You're always on duty.'

She sighed softly. 'Oh, Jamie, I'm sorry. I'll have to make sure I can come to your Nativity play.'

'You must,' he said determinedly.

'I will.' It was a promise, and one she vowed would not be broken.

Running upstairs, she showered quickly, blow-dried her hair and pulled on a sweater-dress in soft lovat-green. She took more than usual care with her make-up as well, and then stood back to examine her handiwork.

She'd do. She didn't have time to worry, because she wanted to read Jamie a story before she went out.

Running downstairs, she found him playing with Beauty on the rug.

'Story?' she said to him, but he shook his head.

'I'm playing with Beauty,' he told her.

There was something, a catch in his voice, that worried her. Was it David?

The doorbell rang, and Jamie jumped to his feet and ran through into the hall. Emily smiled, thinking he was running to answer the door, but then she heard his feet on the stairs and realised he'd run up to his room.

Why?

She opened the door. 'Come in—I must just go and talk to Jamie; he's being funny.'

She left him there and went up to his room. He was sitting at the desk playing with a model, his back definitely towards her.

'That's David,' she told him.

'OK.'

I'll see you later. We won't be very late.'

'OK.'

She crossed over and kissed him, but he didn't react. With a sigh she went downstairs.

'OK?'

She shrugged. 'He said so—several times. It was all I could get out of him.'

'Maybe he's missing his parents.'

'Very likely. I'm ready, if you want to go.'

'Sure?'

She nodded. 'Yes. He's all right. I'll talk to him later.'

They went to a pub—not the Bull, by mutual consent, but another pub further away with a restaurant licence and an excellent reputation.

The meal was wonderful, and for once they kept their conversation strictly off medical matters. He made her laugh, and took her mind off Mr Remington and his threatening behaviour, the Wellcomes, and Jamie.

By the time they left, she had laughed herself silly

and they went out to the car with their arms round each other, still laughing.

When they pulled up outside his cottage and went inside, however, the laughter faded, replaced by need.

'Coffee?' he asked, his voice husky.

'No.'

Their eyes met and desire arced between them.

'Come on,' he murmured, holding out his hand, and he led her upstairs to his bedroom and slowly, methodically, he undressed her, kissing every single inch as it was revealed.

By the time he peeled away the last stocking, she could barely stand. Her fingers trembling, she tugged off his tie, fumbling with the top few buttons and then giving up.

'Pull it over your head,' she told him in an unsteady voice, and as he did so she pressed her lips to the smooth, sleek muscles of his chest. Soft hairs teased her lips, and she burrowed between them and caught one flat male nipple between her teeth.

He groaned and pulled her against him, pressing her against his hips.

She eased away and turned her attention to his trousers, undoing first the belt, then the trouser bar and then the zip, the slow, deliberate rasp scraping on their senses.

'Damn, woman,' he muttered, and she smiled, a secret woman's smile.

Calm now, recovering her poise and enjoying her power, she slid one finger inside the waist of his briefs and ran it round, tormentingly, against the flat wall of his abdomen. It jerked under her hand, tensing, and she turned her palm flat against the warm skin and slid it down, cupping him.

A low oath caught on his breath, and he dropped his head into her shoulder and sighed.

'That feels wonderful.'

'Mmm.'

She moved her hand, tormenting him, and his hips jerked involuntarily. He reached down and shackled her wrist, ending the torment, and met her eyes.

His were smoky with desire, lazy, predatory. Shucking off his remaining clothes, he lifted her and placed her in the centre of the bed.

'You want to play games? We'll play games.'

He nearly drove her crazy, but in the end he lost his control, too, and they tumbled over the edge together, their hearts thrashing in time, locked firmly in each other's arms.

She roused herself as soon as she could bear to.

'I have to go back to Jamie,' she told him.

'He'll be asleep.'

'I know, but if he wakes up—sometimes if he's a bit funny like this he has nightmares. I should be there.'

'OK.'

He kissed her, his lips lingering, and then reluctantly eased away.

They dressed quickly, in silence, and once back at her cottage she didn't invite him in.

'Thank you for a lovely evening,' she said softly, leaning over to kiss him. 'It's been wonderful.'

'It has, hasn't it? We must do it again—soon.'

'Yes—yes, we must.'

She watched him drive away, then went upstairs, her heart light. Maybe, just maybe, it was going to work after all. Jamie would have a father figure, and the baby——Her hand slid to her baby, and a slow smile blossomed on her lips. She would tell him tomorrow.

She went into her room to find Jamie sitting in the middle of her bed, wide-eyed and reproachful.

'I had a dream,' he told her. 'It woke me up, and you weren't here.'

His accusation cut her to the heart. 'Oh, darling, I'm sorry. What was it about?'

He slid off the bed. 'It doesn't matter. I don't like you going out with David. I want you here, with me. I don't like it when you're out.'

'We were only gone for a little while, Jamie,' she reasoned, but her heart was breaking.

'I needed you,' he told her stubbornly. 'I don't want you to go out with him.'

He walked away, his head down, leaving her in the middle of her shattered dream.

CHAPTER NINE

EMILY'S first instinct was to phone David immediately and talk to him, but she had only dialled the first few digits before she thought better of it.

She would give Jamie time to settle, talk to him, see how he really felt. Then she'd talk to David.

How Jamie really felt was clear the following morning. He was subdued, and asked her several times if she was going out with David that night.

'No,' she told him each time.

'Tomorrow?' he asked.

'No. No, I won't be going out with him tomorrow either,' she assured the worried child, and was rewarded by a wobbly smile.

'I love you,' she told him, and he flung himself into her arms and hugged her desperately.

During a break in the day she nipped back and had a word with Mrs Bradley.

'He was ever so upset when you weren't here,' the older woman told her. 'I didn't think I'd be able to console him.'

She gave a wavering smile. 'So that's that, then. I rather thought it was too good to be true.'

'Perhaps he just needs more time to adjust.'

'Perhaps.'

Emily thought it was possible, and so decided still to say nothing to David, other than that Jamie had been upset and they should avoid going out in the evening for a while.

At first she thought he was going to argue, but then his mouth curved in a rueful smile. 'You're his mother. We'll play it your way.'

So easy.

Mr Remington was less so. A couple of days passed, and then the practice receved a letter from his solicitor.

'Stupid man,' Laurence grumbled.

'He's doing what he thinks is right for his daughter,' Emily reasoned, and Laurence gave a startled snort of laughter.

'You're being very philosophical considering it's you he's trying to lampoon.'

'I just know how I would feel,' she said, but couldn't explain any further. It was just a sort of gut feeling, to do with being a parent—not that she was doing so well at that, she thought with a pang.

And she still had to tell David about the baby.

Mrs Richardson came back for her Norplant implant, and Emily did it under the watchful eye of Laurence Allen, who had performed the procedure many times in the past year since it had been available. Although she had done it herself, it had been before Philip became very ill and she had given up her job, and she just felt more confident with Laurence there, too.

Having infiltrated the skin with lignocaine, Emily made a shallow two-millimetre cut in the skin on the inside of Amy's upper arm and inserted six tiny rods impregnated with the contraceptive hormone under the skin in a fan shape. It was all over in less than quarter of an hour, and Amy was thrilled.

'That's brilliant,' she said delightedly as they finished. 'Now I can't possibly forget to take it!'

'Just think long and hard before you let the bomb go off again,' Emily told her as she left.

'I will. This time, at least, someone's going to have to pull the pin, so to speak. It makes it more conscious, and a little harder to be so indiscriminate. Children are so precious, I truly think they ought to be really wanted. Not that ours aren't, of course—even the accidents, which outnumber the planned ones now!'

Emily laughed with her, then turned, her hand automatically lowering to her baby. Wanted? Oh, yes. . .

'Are you OK?' Laurence asked.

She jumped. She had forgotten the other doctor's presence, and snatched her hand away from her abdomen as if she'd been scalded. 'Yes, I'm fine. Just a twinge. Right, I'd better clear up in here. Thank you for your support.'

'You're welcome. Do you feel happy doing it now?'

'Oh, yes.'

'Good. Look, about Clare Remington.'

Emily sighed. 'Yes?'

'I'll go and see her father again, see if we can't defuse this before it goes any further.'

'Do you want me to go?'

He shook his head. 'No. I think he finds your behaviour with David—questionable.'

Emily flushed, but Laurence was undeterred.

'Ignore him. You have a right to your private life. This town is too small for secrets, Emily, but you mustn't let that stop you in your search for happiness.'

She swallowed, and blinked away the tears that

threatened. 'I'll bear that in mind,' she said unsteadily, and busied herself with the debris of the minor operation.

Little did Laurence know that there would be nothing in the way of secrets to keep from now on, she thought sadly.

David appeared at her elbow. 'Are you finished?'

She nodded. 'Yes, why?'

'I've got an hour for lunch, so have you.'

'So?'

'So come home with me.'

'David, it's the middle of the day!' she murmured in protest.

'So? I need you, Em. I want to hold you.'

'I can't.'

'Why?'

'Because.'

'Because what?'

Her shoulders drooped in defeat, her need too great for her fragile self-control. 'I'll follow you,' she told him with a rueful smile.

He left her, and when she'd finished clearing up she drove to his cottage.

He opened the door and pulled her into his arms, his mouth coming down hard on hers. After an age he lifted his head. 'I've missed you,' he muttered.

'It's only been three days.'

'I've still missed you.'

He led her upstairs and made love to her with savage urgency, as if he knew he was losing her, and she clung to him and blinked away the tears.

'I love you,' he whispered in her ear. 'Remember that.'

She said nothing. Her heart was too full, her throat clogged with tears.

She eased away from him and slipped off the bed.

'Where are you going?'

'To shower.'

'No!'

She turned, shocked out of her own sadness by the pain in his voice. 'David? What's wrong?'

His face was tortured, showing his feelings for perhaps the very first time. 'You always do it,' he rasped. 'As soon as we make love, you rush to the shower, as if you can't bear to have any trace of me on you.'

Stunned, she walked back to him. 'That's not true——'

'Isn't it? It damn well feels like it.'

She knelt on the bed, her hand cupping his cheek. 'No—no, that isn't it at all.'

He gripped her wrist. 'What, then?'

She flushed. 'It's for you—I don't want you to feel that I'm. . .'

'What? Loved? For God's sake, Emily, can't you imagine how I feel, how I felt for years, watching you run away as soon as we've made love to scour yourself, as if you feel contaminated by me, by my touch, by my body. . .?'

She dropped her head forward. 'No! Oh, darling, no!' She reached out her other hand and caressed his face, forcing herself to hold those tortured eyes. 'I just—I don't want to offend you——'

'Offend me?' He reached for her. 'You don't offend me, you couldn't. Let me love you.'

'But I——'

'Please?'

She lowered herself to his side, feeling the warmth of his arms encompass her. She touched his shoulder, revelling in the smooth, soft skin over firm muscle.

'I'm sorry I hurt you,' she whispered.

'Forget it.' His voice was gruff, his hands warm and strong. The sweet, musky scent of their loving drifted between them, inflaming her.

'Love me,' she pleaded, her heart breaking.

'I do—until the end of time.'

This time he was slow and gentle, his body calling to hers, and when they reached that tender, glorious peak in harmony her tears refused to be held back.

'Emily?'

She turned her face into his shoulder and bit her lip to hold down the sob, but he wouldn't be shut out. Gripping her chin in tender fingers, he turned her face up to his, searching her tear-filled eyes.

'Darling, what is it? What's wrong?'

'Jamie doesn't want me to see you any more.'

His body jerked, a fine tremor like a small electric shock, but she felt it all the way to her bones.

'What did he say? I thought we were getting on well.'

'So did I. He's decided he doesn't like me going out with you. I thought he might get over it, but I asked him last night if he would mind us going out perhaps next weekend, and he stuck his chin out and his lip wobbled and I didn't have the heart——' Her tears came again in a rush, and David's hands curved protectively round her and cradled her against his chest.

'Ah, love—is this goodbye, then? Our swansong? Is that what you're telling me?'

She tipped her head back and stared into his eyes. 'It has to be,' she said brokenly.

His eyes slammed shut, a single tear squeezed out between his lids, falling on her face.

'David?'

'I'm OK. I knew it was coming. You'd better go back—I'll follow you in a bit.'

He went into the bathroom and turned on the shower, and she dressed quickly and left.

What a time to tell him, she thought, right in the middle of a busy working day, with no opportunity to discuss it.

Still, perhaps that was for the best.

The rest of the day was hectic, and when she emerged from her evening surgery she was told he had gone up to the hospital because he was on duty that evening.

Sue watched her curiously, but she refused to allow herself to be drawn into a discussion. She knew she looked terrible, and, if her last glimpse of David was anything to go by, so did he.

She went home, cuddled her son and the puppy in front of the fire and tried to hide her misery until she was alone in her bed and could let the tears fall.

The weekend was busy. She was on call, and spent the Saturday and Sunday mornings at the hospital running an emergency surgery and casualty clinic combined, followed by a quick check round the wards before going home.

On Sunday afternoon, shortly after they had finished lunch, the phone rang.

'Emily? It's Maureen Whitaker at the hospital. I

wonder if you could come back? I've got Clare Remington here—she's slashed her wrists.'

That was all Emily needed—a potential suicide to muddy the already fraught waters. She rang Laurence before she left, apologised for disturbing him on Sunday and asked if he could meet her at the hospital.

'I just get the feeling this could drive the father over the brink,' she told him.

He agreed to go straight there, and she left immediately.

When she arrived, it was to find a silent and grim-lipped father and daughter sitting in the waiting area.

They both stood up, but she wanted to deal with Clare alone.

'I wonder if you'd mind waiting out here?' she asked Mr Remington with no great hope that he would co-operate.

To her amazement he sat back down and carried on staring at the floor.

She led Clare through into a treatment-room, sat her down and held her hand.

'So what happened?'

'He said I couldn't see Colin again. I love him—you don't know what it's like!'

Emily did know. She knew exactly what it was like.

'Let me see, love,' she coaxed gently, and took the temporary dressings off the wrists. They were only slightly cut, one more than the other, and it was definitely a cry for help rather than a serious attempt to take her life, for which Emily was profoundly grateful.

Her left wrist needed a couple of stitches, but the right, presumably cut last with the weakened left hand,

she just cleaned up and dressed while the local anaesthetic took effect.

'What did your father say?' she asked as she gently
drew the edges of the wound together.

'Nothing. He just covered my wrists, put me in the
car and drove me here. He hasn't said a word to me.'

Just then there was a kerfuffle in the waiting-room
and the door was pushed open.

'Clare? What happened?'

A young man in jeans and a denim jacket crouched
beside Clare, taking her hands tenderly in his and
staring down at her wrists. 'Why?' he asked, his face
tortured.

'He wouldn't let me see you. He said I couldn't see
you again.'

The youth's face worked, and then he lowered his
lips to her hand and kissed it. 'Silly girl,' he muttered.
'I'm not worth this.'

'You are to me.'

'Oh, God,' he groaned, his voice cracking, and,
wrapping his arms around her, he hugged her tight.

'I don't want to interfere,' Emily said wryly, 'but do
you suppose I could finish putting in this last suture
before you get carried away?'

Flushing, he released her and straightened up, his
hand on Clare's shoulder offering silent support while
Emily knotted the silk and snipped the stitch off, then
dressed it. 'There. Now I'll have a word with your
father, and you can go.'

She left them alone together while she sought out
Mr Remington, but Laurence had arrived by this time
and had wheeled him off to Maureen's office. He

beckoned to Emily through the glass, and she went through and joined them.

'How is she?' Mr Remington asked.

'She'll be fine. It was relatively superficial. A cry for help rather than a serious attempt to do away with herself, but I would take it seriously if I were you.'

He nodded. 'I will. I think it's time we sat down and had a really serious talk. Maybe she's old enough now for this relationship, maybe not. My gut reaction is still not, but perhaps I ought to start really listening to her.' He swallowed, and forced himself to meet her eyes.

'I owe you an apology. I realise now that what you did was the best option in difficult circumstances, and I know you didn't prescribe the Pill for her lightly. I just assumed you dished them out like dolly mixtures, but obviously you don't. You care—perhaps more obviously than I do. And you listened—which I didn't. Thank you.'

Emily was completely taken aback. She had expected another assault on her integrity, and instead there was a complete retraction and apology.

She made the appropriate noises and went back out to find Clare and her boyfriend. Mr Remington followed her out of the room and stood staring at the lad for some time, then extended his hand. 'Colin—perhaps you'd like to come back and have some tea with us.'

Clare's face lit up. 'Oh, Dad, thanks,' she said, and threw herself into his arms.

'I don't approve, mind,' he told her warningly. 'We are going to sit down, all of us, and have a good, long, serious talk.'

Emily and Laurence watched them leave, then turned to each other and smiled.

'Well, fancy that.'

'Fancy. End of court case.'

She laughed with relief. 'Thank God.' She glanced at her watch. 'I'd better get home.'

Laurence's hand on her arm stopped her. 'Are you OK?'

She didn't pretend not to understand. 'I'll live.'

He nodded, and without another word she turned and left.

Clare came to see her on the following Friday to have her stitches out of her wrist, and she told Emily she was coming off the Pill.

'Dad says we're both very young and we've got our whole lives ahead of us. He says we can still see each other, but only supervised and in company, and not too often. Then if we still feel the same in a year's time we can think again.'

'How do you feel about that?' Emily asked her, concerned that if it wasn't the girl's wishes she would find a way to be with Colin without supervision—and with possibly disastrous consequences.

'I think he might be right,' she said, a touch sheepishly.

Emily smiled, truly relieved. 'I'm so glad—glad you're talking to your parents, glad they're listening to you, glad you and Colin have decided to be sensible. You are still terribly young for such a serious commitment, and if it isn't that serious you really shouldn't be making love.'

Clare blushed and dropped her eyes. 'I know that now. I didn't realise before. It's very special, isn't it?'

Emily felt a lump in her throat. 'Yes, Clare, it is—or it should be. There, your arm will be fine now. Look after yourself—and if you change your mind for goodness' sake come back first!'

She smiled. 'I will. Thank you for being so kind. I'm sorry Dad got all bent out of shape.'

'I think he had a right. I think if you'd been my daughter I might have got all bent out of shape too.'

They exchanged a smile of understanding, and Emily watched her go. A success story? Hopefully.

She finished her surgery and went into the common-room to find Laurence to tell him the news. He wasn't there, but David was, and her footsteps faltered.

'Hi,' he said softly.

'Hi. I was looking for Laurence.'

'He's gone home.'

'Oh.' She twisted her wedding-ring. 'Well, I suppose I should be leaving too——'

'Emily?'

She turned back to him.

'Are you happy here?'

'Happy?' she asked numbly.

'Yes. If it weren't for me, I mean, messing things up for you. Are you happy in the practice, in Biddlecombe, at the cottage? Is Jamie happy?'

'Yes—yes to all of them. Why?'

His shoulders lifted slightly. 'I just wondered.'

'David. . .?' She hesitated.

'Yes?'

'I—nothing. I'll go home.'

She turned away, unable to stand the pain he was

trying to hide. Of course she was happy, happier than she had been for years—or would have been, had Jamie not come between them so effectively.

She would have to talk to him again, try and sound him out a little further. Once he was used to the idea of David in their lives, perhaps he would accept it more readily.

She hoped so, quite desperately, because one thing she was sure of—without David she was nothing. Far from messing it up, his presence in her life had brought back a meaning to it that had been missing for eight long, lonely years.

But enough was enough. What was it Mrs T had said? 'Seems to me a great waste of being alive if you don't bother to learn from your mistakes.'

Well, she had learnt from hers. David was more important to her than anything else, and she wasn't going to give up on him again. She would talk to Jamie, and, please God, he would learn to love David as she had.

The alternative didn't bear thinking about.

CHAPTER TEN

EMILY wanted to wait for the right moment to talk to Jamie—but, like all right moments, it came when it was least expected.

It was late on Sunday afternoon, and Beauty was playing with a ball, dashing after it and then running into the corner with it to chew it, much to Jamie's chagrin. He was trying to teach her to fetch, and she was being thoroughly difficult.

'I wonder if David could teach her?' he said thoughtfully. 'Bridie and Ruffian fetch.'

Emily's heart crashed against her ribs.

'Would you like him to try?' she asked cautiously.

'Mmm—do you think he would?'

'We can certainly ask him. Of course,' she added casually, 'if we aren't seeing him, he can't really train her.'

'But he could,' the boy said absently, wrestling the ball from Beauty and rolling it again. 'Fetch, Beauty, good girl—oh, no! She's done it again!'

He turned to Emily, laughing. 'David will *have* to do it—I'm hopeless.'

Emily patted the sofa beside her. 'Jamie, come here for a minute, sweetheart. I want to talk to you.'

He wriggled up beside her and snuggled under her arm. 'What's wrong?'

'Nothing—well, not really. I wanted to talk to you about David.'

'He hasn't been here for ages—doesn't he like me any more?'

She blinked. 'I thought you didn't want us to see so much of him.'

'What? Why do you think that?'

'You said so. You said you didn't like me going out with him——'

'I don't. I don't like it when you go out to work either, but you have to do that, so it's OK. I like David, though. He's really nice.' He paused for a moment, then added thoughtfully, 'He's a bit like Dad.'

Emily hugged him gently, hardly able to believe what he was saying. 'Yes, he is, a bit,' she agreed, trying hard to keep her voice steady. 'Jamie, how would you feel about having David as a sort of dad?'

'Like you're my mum now?'

She nodded.

'That would be really cool, Emmy! I could ride the donkey, and play with Bridie and Ruffian—do you think he'd want to?'

Emily wanted to cry. She felt the tears pricking behind her eyes and blinked rapidly. Could it really be so easy? 'Yes, Jamie, I think he might,' she told him.

'He'll have to ask you, though—girls can't ask boys that sort of thing. It isn't right.'

She bit her lip to stop the smile. 'Then I'll have to make very sure he knows to ask the question, won't I?' she said seriously.

Her first opportunity to talk to David was on Monday, but the surgery was crowded, patients were waiting and it was not a very good time. Anyway, she found she was suddenly nervous.

'Can I see you later?' she asked, surprised by the slight tremor in her voice.

He looked serious. 'I was going to ask you the same thing. How about lunchtime, at my place?'

She nodded. 'Fine—thanks. I'll see you about one.'

'Fine.' He walked away, and she noticed the tension in his shoulders. She would have to rub them later—once she'd given him the necessary lead to pop the question. . .

She went back to her consulting-room and called the first patient.

It was a girl of about twelve, who was listless and had a slight fever. She was complaining of a sore armpit, and on examination Emily found her lymph glands were swollen. She checked her throat, all other glands and her spleen, but could find nothing wrong in any other area.

Odd, she thought, and then noticed a tiny, healed scratch on the girl's hand, the same side as the swollen glands. At the end of the scratch was a small, swollen papule, like a blister.

Emily looked at it, then turned to the child.

'Have you been scratched by a cat recently?' she asked.

'A cat—no, I don't think so,' her mother replied.

'Yes, I was—at Susie's house the other day. Fluffy scratched me.'

'Oh, yes—but that was ages ago—the beginning of last week.'

Emily nodded. 'That's right. I think you've got a thing called cat scratch disease. It's caused by a bacteria—we don't know which one yet, but it makes the nearest glands swell, and sometimes there's a slight temperature and a general feeling of being unwell.'

'That's just how I feel,' the girl told her.

'There you are, then. Problem solved. Nothing nasty, nothing to worry about. I'll give you some antibiotics to clear up the infection in your lymph glands and you'll be fine. All right?'

They left, clutching their prescription and a new body of knowledge, and Emily smiled to herself. Thank goodness she had noticed the scratch!

It was obviously hand day, she thought a couple of patients later, because a lady with a sore, itchy rash on both hands came in.

'Look at me!' she exclaimed, pulling up both sleeves. 'I look as if I'm wearing gloves!'

Emily looked carefully at the skin, and saw a fine, diffuse rash over the whole area. In places it was coming up in vesicles and beginning to scale.

'It must be my new oven cleaner,' she said crossly. 'I knew they were dangerous!'

'Did you wear rubber gloves?'

'Of course! Lot of good it's done me; it's just soaked straight through!'

'No,' Emily assured her. 'It's the rubber gloves themselves. You've got allergic contact dermatitis.'

'From the rubber?'

'Yes, I think so. Were they a new brand?'

'Well—I don't normally wear them at all, so I bought them especially to do the oven.'

Emily nodded. 'Don't worry, it'll soon clear up. I'll give you some Betnovate cream to rub on the rash, and some antihistamine tablets to take to subdue the itching. Do you get drowsy if you take Piriton?'

'I don't know, I've never taken it, but it doesn't matter. I don't have to drive or operate machinery—well, only the Hoover.'

Emily smiled. 'That's OK, then. Here, take these as directed and you'll soon notice an improvement.'

'I'll tell you one good thing,' the woman said as she stood up to go. 'My husband'll have to clean the oven from now on.'

Emily chuckled. Every cloud, and all that. She glanced at her watch as the woman left.

Ten-fifteen. Two and a quarter hours to go.

Her stomach was fizzing, her heart pounding.

'Don't worry, baby,' she told her child. 'We'll soon get all this straightened out and then we can be a real family.'

She pressed the buzzer for the next patient, and carried on with her surgery.

At eleven she went out into the office to ask Sue for another packet of prescription stationery for the computer, and found she wasn't there. She checked the usual place under the counter, but there wasn't any.

'I wonder where she keeps it?' Emily muttered to herself, and she turned to the desk to leave Sue a note.

As she did so, a letter caught her eye. It was to a professional journal, and was asking for an insertion in the 'Partners Wanted' column. Attached to the letter was an advert. She read it, her lips moving as she did so.

'Partner wanted in rural North Devon practice. Must be qualified in minor surgery. . .' blah, blah '. . .ability to map read. . .' Damn! My job! They've decided to get rid of me, and they haven't even told me! I've got two more months!'

Rage boiled over, fuelled by her anxiety over David and her uncertain future. She grabbed the paper and stalked down the corridor to the common-room, throwing open the door.

Laurence and Robin were in there, and she marched up to Laurence and thrust the letter under his nose.

'What the hell is this?' she demanded ungraciously. 'You might at least have had the decency to tell me you wouldn't be keeping me on at the end of my trial period before you placed the damned advert!'

Laurence came slowly to his feet, his eyes searching her face.

'It's not your job, Emily.'

'What? But of course it is. Who else's?'

He let his breath out slowly. 'David's.

She felt her blood run cold. 'David's?' she whispered.

'Hasn't he said anything?'

'No—no, not a thing. When did he. . .?'

'The weekend. I thought you knew.'

She shook her head, unable to believe it. 'I had no idea.'

'You'd better go and talk to him. He's at home now.'

'But—I've got visits to make.'

'I'll do them.'

She swallowed. 'Sue's got the list. Laurence, are you sure?'

He nodded. 'Go on. I'll see you later.'

She turned on her heel and ran back to her surgery, grabbing her bag and keys before running out through the waiting-room to the car park.

She drove to his cottage as if the hounds of hell were after her, which indeed she felt they were.

His car was outside, and she pulled up behind it and got out, running to the door.

Once there, her courage deserted her. What could she say? How could she persuade him to stay?

The door swung open before she touched the bell. He eyed her for a moment, then stood back. 'You know,' he said flatly. 'I was going to tell you at lunchtime.'

'Why?' she asked. 'You can't leave me—not now. Where are you going?'

'I don't know. Cornwall, perhaps? I just know I can't stay here being torn apart like this any longer. You're settled, Jamie's settled—it makes sense that it's me.' He paused for a moment, then his hand came out and brushed her cheek. 'I'll miss you.'

'No,' she said firmly.

'I will, Emily.'

'No, you won't, because you won't be going anywhere without me. Not if I have anything to do with it.'

He turned away. 'Don't be daft. Even without the problem of Jamie, what have I got to offer you? You've got a better house than I have, more money than I could ever dream of earning in a lifetime, and without me to mess things up you could be happy.'

She almost stamped her foot. 'Would you just listen to me for a minute? The house is neither here nor there, all Philip's money is in trust for Jamie, except Mrs Bradley's wages and a small amount for untoward necessities. I have nothing—a few hundred pounds in savings, that's all. And Jamie——'

She swallowed and touched his rigid shoulder, the temper going out of her voice. 'Jamie would like you to train the puppy to fetch.'

He turned slowly towards her. 'What?'

She smiled tentatively. 'Jamie told me last night that he likes you. He thinks you're a lot like his father, and he'd like you to be a sort of father to him, the way I'm a sort of mother. He didn't like you taking me out because he doesn't like it when I go out, not because he doesn't like you. He doesn't like me going out to work either, but that isn't going to be a problem soon because I'm going to have to give up, because of the baby—if you'll agree to support me, that is.'

David stared at her, his face uncomprehending.

'Baby?' he croaked. 'What baby?'

'Our baby—the baby we started the night I crashed the car.'

A puzzled frown crossed his face, then a smile started deep in his eyes, in among the tears. 'A baby? We're going to have a baby?'

'Yes—and in this town that could be a problem, so unless you want me to be the object of considerable gossip you'd better ask me the question Jamie says I'm not allowed to ask you, and we'd better get on with it.'

'Are you all right?'

'That's not the question,' she told him softly, moved by the wonder on his face.

He laughed, a tiny, incredulous chuckle, followed by a full, deep belly laugh. It was cut off abruptly as he tugged her into his arms and crushed her against his chest.

'Oh, Emily—marry me, for God's sake—now, today.'

'I can't. It's too soon.'

'It can't be too soon for me.'

'No, but there's the small matter of the law.'

He laughed again and leant back to look down into her eyes.

'Who cares about the law?'

'I do. I want this marriage to be a proper one.'

He was suddenly sober. 'So do I,' he said, with deep sincerity. 'It's going to work, Emily. Trust me. We'll make it work—for everybody's sake.'

He lowered his lips to hers, and as the passion rocked them he lifted her carefully and carried her to his room. There he made love to her, with infinite care and tenderness, and when it was over he cradled her against his side.

'Now, about this wedding,' he murmured against her hair.

'Mmm?'

'How about Friday?' he suggested.

'No. It's Jamie's Nativity play. He's a shepherd and I promised I'd be there.'

'Monday, then.'

'That's our wedding anniversary.'

He looked down at her. 'Is that a good omen or a bad one?'

She smiled. 'I don't know. Are you superstitious? It would have been our thirteenth.'

'Perhaps it would bring us luck this time. It would keep it tidy,' he said with a smile. 'Only one date to remember—you might get a bunch of flowers on the right day if I had two reasons to remember it.'

She laughed softly. 'That would be a first.'

'There'll be lots of firsts, I promise. Trust me, Emily. This time we'll make it work.'

David went to the hospital the following morning to see Joe Hardwill among others.

He sounded his chest and found it clearer, at last, and then checked his lower leg for tenderness and mobility of the ankle.

'How's the physio going?'

'All right. I can get about now without crutches. Time to be going home soon, I fancy.'

'Yes, I think so.' He pulled the pyjama leg down and stood up slowly. 'Joe, do you remember when we were talking about the new doctor, back in September, and you said there might be a bit of love interest?' he said as he straightened.

Joe's twinkling eyes searched David's face. 'Popped the question, boy?'

David grinned. 'Yes, I have.'

'So when's the big day?'

'Monday—if the vicar can fit us in.'

He nodded. 'Bit of a hurry, eh?'

David's grin became sheepish. 'Well, there are two reasons for the hurry. One of them is that it's our original wedding anniversary.'

Joe nodded. 'I'd heard about that. The Miles girl left her the cottage, didn't she?'

'Yes.'

'The other reason I can guess,' Joe said with a wheezy chuckle. 'Still, after so many years I reckon it's about time.'

David patted him on the shoulder. 'I think you're right, Joe—I think you're right.'

They saw the vicar together at lunchtime, and although he was a little surprised he nevertheless agreed to marry them in the church in Biddlecombe on Monday, at the exact time of their first wedding.

'It's a sort of action replay,' David told the vicar, 'only this time we're going to do it right.'

The vicar nodded, and then went through the details of the special licence with them.

There was no question of doing it quietly, of course. Everyone who came into the surgery had an opinion, and expressed it freely.

All were pleased, but a great many thought it was desperately romantic and a few were bold enough to say it was about time, the way they'd been carrying on.

Emily, who thought they'd been very discreet, hid her blushes and did her best to ignore them all. David, who was far better known and definitely much loved by his patients, was teased mercilessly. He took it in good part, however, and just hoped none of them would find out about the baby.

They went together to Jamie's Nativity play on Friday, and then Emily went home to her parents in Oxford for the weekend and dug out her old wedding-dress from the back of the wardrobe. It still fitted as it had when she had first worn it—slightly better, perhaps, with the fullness of maturity—and they took it to a dry-cleaners and collected it two hours later, good as new.

'Are you sure, darling?' her mother asked her over and over again. 'He hurt you so badly before.'

'I hurt him, too,' Emily assured her. 'We were too young. We're older now, and wiser. Anyway, there's another reason.'

Her mother's eyes widened. 'Emily! You're a doctor—how could you be so silly?'

She laughed. 'Silly? I thought you wanted to be a grandmother.'

'Well, I do, but—you aren't marrying him just for the baby, are you?'

'No,' she assured her emphatically. 'Definitely not.'

Two hundred miles away, David was having the same conversation with his parents.

'Should have thought you'd know better,' Bill said crisply. 'Well, you'll have to take it seriously this time—no mucking about, not with children involved.'

'I'll take it seriously, Dad. I love her, I always did. And this time I'll make sure we both remember it.'

Monday dawned cold, wet and windy. By eleven o'clock, however, the wind had blown away most of the cloud and the sun was out, gleaming on the wet rooftops and bringing colour to the winter landscape.

Emily's mother helped her to dress, and Mrs Bradley sorted Jamie out. He was a page boy—not in all that 'cissy stuff', as he put it, but in a new suit, with a proper tie, and a carnation in his buttonhole.

David had sent the buttonhole together with a bouquet of red roses for Emily—thirteen, one for every year since their marriage.

They drove down to the church in her parents' car, Emily perched in the back trying not to crumple her wedding-dress, and Mrs Bradley and Jamie each side of her holding up her veil.

As the clock on the town hall struck twelve, Emily

stepped out of the car, straightened her veil and smiled at her mother and Mrs Bradley.

'You'd better go in,' she told them.

Her father tucked her hand in his arm and smiled down at her. 'All set?'

She nodded. 'Jamie, are you all right, darling?'

'Yes.'

He looked nervous, and she felt a moment of panic. What if he changed his mind?

She heard the organist strike up the first notes of 'Here Comes the Bride', and, tightening her grip on her father's arm, she walked calmly through the door and down the aisle.

David was standing there, his broad back towards her, his hair gleaming mahogany in a stray beam of sunlight. His brother was beside him, identical save for the darker hair, and he turned and winked.

She walked past old friends and loved ones: Philip's parents, beaming delightedly and winking at Jamie, Mrs Bradley at their side; Emily's mother, a handkerchief at the ready; the Trevellyans, behind David.

And then she was there, standing by his side, and he turned to look at her. She felt his strength pouring into her, his love, his steadfastness, and a smile touched her lips.

Suddenly his jacket was tugged from behind and he turned, puzzled.

'You will bring Ruffian and Bridie to live with us, won't you?' Jamie stage-whispered.

David nodded.

'And train Beauty?'

He nodded again. 'Yes—I promise.'

'OK.' He grinned, and his face screwed up in a wink.

David returned the wink and knuckled his hair, then turned back to the vicar, a broad smile on his face.

'I think we're ready now,' he said softly.

The vicar cleared his throat and raised his hands to the congregation.

'Dearly beloved, we are gathered here together. . .'

As Emily listened to the familiar words, she thought back over the past thirteen years. So many mistakes, so many things they had left undone, so many times they had turned away from a difficult problem. Instead of talking it through, they had rowed, stalked away from each other and then made up later without exchanging a word to resolve the initial conflict.

Never again. They would row, she knew that. But they would talk about what worried them, sort out their differences, respect each other's opinions.

As David made his vows, his voice clear and steady, his eyes locked with hers, she felt a deep and enduring peace steal over her heart.

And as he took his ring from her finger and handed it to the vicar for the blessing, then returned it to her she felt a sense of rightness in her world that had been missing for eight long years.

'I now pronounce you man and wife,' the vicar said. 'Those whom God has joined together let no man put asunder.'

'They won't,' David vowed softly, and lifting her veil, he bent his head and brushed her lips.

'Is that all I get?' she whispered.

'Hussy,' he mumbled, and, dragging her into his arms, he kissed her soundly.

She heard a sniff—her mother, or David's?

Or both?

And behind them Jamie, quite distinctly, said, 'Yuck!'

David threw another log on the fire. 'Hungry?' he asked.

'No—how about some champagne?'

His eyes gleamed in the firelight. 'Just what I was thinking.'

He disappeared to the kitchen, returning moments later with two glasses and an open bottle.

'It was good of your parents to do this for us twice,' he said with a smile, handing her a glass.

'I think they were glad to—anything rather than have an illegitimate grandchild.'

He chuckled, and, sitting on the rug by the fire, he propped his back against the chair and patted the rug between his legs. She bunched up her wedding-dress and sat down, leaning back against his chest.

'Mmm. This brings back memories.'

'It's meant to. How are you feeling?'

'Oh, I feel wonderful.'

He slid his hand over her still flat tummy and sighed. 'You do, don't you?' He nuzzled her neck, the slight scrape of his beard doing amazing things to her nerve-endings.

'Sexy beast—you'll slop my champagne.'

'Mmm—you don't need it anyway, not when you're pregnant. Give it to me.'

He put it down, then turned her in his arms.

'Do you know what I'm going to do?'

She shook her head, laughter brimming in her eyes.

'I can't imagine.'

A sly smile crept on to his face, and his hand found

the tiny buttons at the back of her dress and slowly, one by one, he unfastened them.

'Oh, you cheeky thing.'

'Mmm. I don't suppose you'd like to strip for me?'

'There was a time,' she told him, 'when you weren't too lazy to undress me yourself.'

He rose to his feet, grasped her hand and drew her up beside him.

'Turn round.'

One by one, slowly, he unfastened the rest of the buttons, laying a trail of fire down her spine with his lips. Her dress slithered down, pooling at her feet, and he held her hand as she stepped out of it.

He threw it on to the sofa and she chided him.

'Careful!'

'Why? You won't need it again.'

A smile bloomed on her face. 'I know.'

Her fingers rose to his tie, tugging it off, then quickly worked the buttons down the front of his shirt, exposing the broad expanse of his chest. Mischievously, she tweaked a hair and he swore softly and grabbed her hand.

'You're in one of those moods, are you?'

She giggled.

'I'm going to have to do something about you. Sit down—just there—and don't move.'

He undressed as she watched, kicking off his shoes, throwing his trousers and shirt after her wedding-dress. Then he knelt in front of her and unclipped her bra, catching the burgeoning fullness of her breasts in his hands.

'Maternity is going to suit you,' he murmured,

lowering his head to the smooth curves, and slowly, lavishly, he paid them homage.

'You were in too much of a hurry thirteen years ago,' she said softly.

'You want to hurry?'

She shook her head. 'No—we don't need to. We've got all the time in the world.'

He lay down and drew her into his arms, cradling her head against his chest.

'I love you, Emily Trevellyan.'

Emily Trevellyan. Funny how absolutely right it sounded.

She lifted her face to his.

'I love you, too—so very much.'

His eyes darkened, the flames burning hotter, and lowered his mouth to hers.

Their prayer for peace had been answered.

EPILOGUE

EMILY heard his key in the door, then the soft slam and his brisk stride on the stairs.

'Hi. All done?'

'God, I should hope so. What a weekend! Have I got time to get back into bed for a cuddle?'

She shook her head. 'No—David, how long does it take to get to Barnstaple?'

His eyes cut into hers. 'About twenty-five minutes. Why?'

'Because I don't think I'm going to make it.'

His eyes widened. 'Have your waters broken?'

She nodded. 'A few minutes ago. And I have this very definite urge to push.'

'Oh, my God.' The blood literally seemed to drain from his face. 'Emily, I'll call the ambulance——'

'What for? I'm fit and healthy, you're a doctor——'

'But it's twins! For God's sake, darling!'

'So? You just have to do it twice.'

'Not at home. Please, Emily. . .'

She shrugged. 'The cottage hospital, then, but we'll have to move very fast.'

'I'd better look at you.'

'No,' she said firmly. 'Just put me in the car and get me there.'

So he did, carrying her carefully down the stairs, fastening her seatbelt awkwardly round her swollen

186

abdomen and then driving like a bat out of hell for the hospital, the green light on his car flashing all the way.

'That's pulling rank,' she told him as he switched the siren on to cut through the early morning traffic in town.

'Damn job has to have some privileges,' he grunted, and swung into the ambulance bay of the hospital, siren still blaring.

Maureen rushed out, took one look at Emily and went back for a trolley.

Minutes later, without bothering to wait for the midwife, their first daughter made her appearance.

David sighed, wiped his brow with the back of his arm and grinned at her weakly. 'One down, one to go.'

She cradled her first-born child against her breast, her eyes filling.

'She's beautiful.'

'She's noisy,' he said, but she noticed his eyes were suspiciously bright.

The midwife arrived at the same time as the second baby, another girl.

'Identical,' she said in satisfaction. 'That'll keep the teachers on their toes in a few years' time.'

David grinned. 'Runs in the family, like wooden legs.'

'Are you a twin?'

He nodded. 'Yes.'

'Oh, well, get's it over with in one fell swoop, I suppose—unless you're going to do an Amy Richardson on us?'

Emily, totally fascinated by her two beautiful daughters, looked up at David and smiled mistily.

'They are so lovely.'

'Are you all right?'

'Never better. Are you?'

He sat down suddenly. 'It's a bit much, all at once.' He dredged up a shaky smile. 'I love you, clever girl.'

She grinned, very pleased with herself. 'I could have had them at home.'

'You damn nearly did. Why didn't you ring me?'

She smiled. 'What, and have you take me all the way to Barnstaple?'

His eyes narrowed. 'You planned this.'

She blinked innocently. 'Me?'

He scowled, then his face softened and he reached out to touch his tiny daughters, still resting against her breasts.

'What are we going to call them?'

'I thought—Sarah,' she said quietly. 'And maybe— Jenny?'

He nodded. 'Yes. Yes, I think so.'

He stood up and bent over her, placing a tender kiss on her brow.

'Well done.' A huge yawn cracked his face. 'Lady, your timing is lousy.'

She grinned mischievously. 'I thought it was rather good, myself.'

'Hmm.'

The midwife took the babies from Emily, one at a time, and washed and dressed them, then put them in David's arms.

'You sit there with your family while Dr Allen sorts your wife out,' she told him, and he settled back in the big armchair with a baby on each side.

They were all asleep in seconds.

Emily, watching him, thought of Sarah and Philip,

and their son, her son now and David's, and of Jenny Wellcome who had died the night the babies were conceived.

If it hadn't been for Sarah dying, Emily might never have come back to Biddlecombe and found David again, and if she hadn't spent the evening at the hospital checking on Jenny she might not have ended up in his arms that night.

Both women, in their way, had been instrumental in her happiness. It seemed fitting that they should be remembered.

Watching her husband and babies now, Emily settled back against the pillow.

Her marriage was working this time, truly working. They had learned a lot between them, and they wouldn't waste this second chance. Once more, she thought, with feeling. . .

 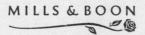

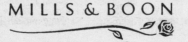

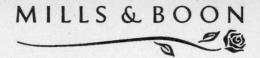

MILLS & BOON